Philip Harper

——

Simon & Schuster

NEW YORK

LONDON

TORONTO

SYDNEY

SINGAPORE

DEATH BENEFIT

A GRAY INVESTIGATIVE THRILLER

SIMON & SCHUSTER
Rockefeller Center
1230 Avenue of the Americas
New York, NY 10020

SIMON & SCHUSTER and colophon are registered trademarks
of Simon & Schuster, Inc.

Designed by Fritz Metsch

Manufactured in the United States of America

1 3 5 7 9 10 8 6 4 2

Library of Congress Cataloging-in-Publication Data

Harper, Philip
   Death benefit : a Gray investigative thriller / Philip Harper
     p. cm
    1. Private investigators—Pennsylvania—Philadelphia—
Fiction. 2. Philadelphia (Pa.)—Fiction. 3. Insurance
crimes—Fiction. I. Title.
PS3558.A62484 D4 2000
813'.54—dc21
                            00-037050

ISBN 0-684-86917-9

A   D E D I C A T I O N :

This book is . . .
for Sue, most of all, who always loves wisely and well.
for Lillian, for her strong love and unyielding support.
for Jesse, whose intelligence and friendship is so bright and true.
for Jon, because no one works and plays harder or brings more joy.
for Mark: "just write," he says, a brother's wisdom and love.
for Dorothy, who wishes Gray and his creators so well.
for the friends of this fine day, John and Linda, Emily and Hank.
for all the days there were and are, Barry and Ellie, Helen and Jon.

A   N O T E :

These books of Gray are fiction, but in every other important way, these stories tell only truths. The methods Gray
uses, the sources of information he finds, the places he goes,
the newspapers he both dismisses and loves, the existence of
the little gods and the damage they do—all these are real.
Ask any experienced investigative reporter. They live with
the burden of knowing.

And a final wish for dead heroes:
a place to live again.
—STUART GREEN

With special thanks to Joe D. and Dara L.

DEATH BENEFIT

C H A P T E R   O N E

His mind raced, as usual, turning information into endless categories and associations. The minty smell of grass. The flat mud and moss of the trees. He looked down and saw dark soil, good for growing. If a man was desperate, he could use the park's resources to make food. Such knowledge was good to have. It would be part of a backup plan, a possible means of escape. Jim Hartman filed it away, along with scores of other backup plans already in place.

He was in Fairmount Park, and he kept his eyes on a particular woman who was in the middle of warming up for a workout. People walked by. He imagined what it would take to bring each one down, visualized himself in action. A footsweep and a wrist-edge blow to the throat. That one, done. Move in close, snap the head up sharply into the man's face. That one, done. A tall man, stronger than him. Jab to the eyes, take away the size advantage. Then use a knife kick. Done. In his head, each conflict began and ended, while he crouched, completely still.

He stood up and stretched his legs, continuing to watch the young blond woman. He needed to be ready to run with her. In recent weeks, he'd been observing her routine. She was compulsive. She used the simple wooden workout stations along the Valley Green path in the park the way others used machines at the gym. She kept increasing her number of sit-ups.

He liked women who worked out so rigorously. He had once made a big play for a woman at a gym after watching her lift for two hours. Getting the date was easy. Making connections was his specialty. He went out with her a few times. He'd liked her enough to let her go, to make nothing out of their relationship that he could use.

But today's woman wasn't picked out at random. This was business. He'd known her for ten years, since she was a kid. He'd sold her parents life insurance, helped them with financial and legal matters, all legitimate, matters of trust. He'd watched the girl grow up. She became a twenty-six-year-old assistant trader on Philadelphia's commodities mart, living on her own in Center City. She had grown up enough to be useful. She was so useful that she had to die.

He casually approached her.

"Mary Cooper?" He sounded a little uncertain, but nice.

"Yes?" she said, polite, without invitation. She was pretty enough to be familiar with chance encounters and where they sometimes led.

"Mary, you don't remember me? Jim Hartman? I've known your parents for years. Insurance. Remember?"

It took her a minute to look at him and to think back through the years. Then recognition came.

"Mr. Hartman, wow. I don't think I've ever seen you without a pin-striped suit."

He smiled at the compliment, subtle as it was. He was forty-nine, but at six feet, with thick dark hair and blue eyes and a slim build, he looked much younger. His appearance always helped him, but then everything did.

"I didn't recognize you either, Mary, not at first. So we're even there." He hesitated, timing it. "You've changed a lot."

She rubbed the sweat off her arms with a light-blue towel. "I'm not a kid anymore, I guess," she said.

"How're your parents? I've been meaning to visit."

"Same as always. They're fine. I see them all the time. But I'm glad I have my own place."

He heard the pride. She was still young enough to make having her own place an accomplishment. She was doing well and that was good. It increased her value. He had pulled her credit history and her medical records, by using the form people signed as part of a life insurance application. Forging her signature was risk-free. No one ever checked that kind of form, especially at a doctor's office. He had scanned the papers with relief.

She was perfect. Occupation, age, and health were the most important variables juries considered in awards for wrongful death. Mary Cooper was in excellent health. She was likely to live a long, productive life. Her lifelong earnings potential was high.

He knew her routine. After sit-ups, she usually ran in the wooded section of the park. She began to stretch.

"If you're going running, that's what I was up to also. I could join you, if that's okay."

She didn't hesitate.

"Sure," she said.

There was nothing like a history with people to make things easier, but at this point it didn't really matter what she said. The plan was now in motion. If she'd turned him down and run off alone, he would have followed her, unseen. He glanced around. It was late afternoon. Some people were out walking on the path near the creek but the area wasn't crowded. She led the way. He followed close behind.

The jogging path took a steep incline. The woods fifty feet

up got dense. They slowly wound upward with the hill. She wasn't a talker. He enjoyed the silent run. She was better adapted than he for running. She handled the changes in terrain like an animal, adjusting her stride, quickening when the way was clear, slowing for rough patches. But he was determined and had no difficulty keeping up.

They went through thick brush for a few minutes, then they came to one of the fieldstone bridges sprinkled throughout the park, leftover city quaintness, markers of Philadelphia past. The bridges were mostly in disrepair, mortar and stones held together by weight and proximity, with some places loosened and worn away.

He took big strides and caught up to her as she came around the edge of the entry road and stepped onto the bridge's slate. They stopped for a moment, both breathing heavily. He drew his arm back and used the short-stroke side-facing punch of a Chinese boxer, his hip turned neatly into the punch, providing the power. His arm relaxed to a whip, fist loose until the contact with her jaw, then it tightened to a knot to capture the force, to carry through the thrust. He stared intently, without emotion. This was his job.

He admired the efficiency of the blow he made. He loved the martial arts. They had always seemed ideal for him—a way to be violent that relied more on preparation and skill than on size or strength, although he had both. The woman was instantly unconscious. He took her in his arms, her body featherweight and soft. The blood was still flowing fast beneath her skin, pulsing from her workout. Her flesh was pale. The flattened stone squares of the bridge sheltered them from surrounding view. He leaned her body against his, ran his hands through her hair, kissed her lightly on the lips. He held her under the arms, walked her a few feet across the stone road, and placed her in the middle of the bridge. Missing bits of mortar and broken slate left gaps in the bridge's bottom. Through them he saw the soft green of the mossy wood and the slight blue trail of slow-moving water ten feet below.

She began to regain consciousness and looked up at him, uncomprehending. He stepped toward her, then turned to the fragmented wall of the bridge. He bent down and felt the muscles of his thighs and knees tighten, his calves taut. He grabbed hold of the edge of an outcropping of stone on the side of the bridge. He pulled in one smooth motion, feeling the dry and weakened mortar yield to his pressure. He uncoiled from his crouch, taking the piece of stone with him. She watched, but was too dazed to move. He stood, tall and straight, the hundred pounds of dead stone weight held up above his head.

"What are you—" she managed to say, her head and shoulders half up off the mortar.

He looked down, the slate's shadow shielding her body from the sky, and then he let go. She yelled, but the sound was gone in a second as the stone scythe moved through her.

He rolled the big piece of stone off the dead woman, then pushed the body off the edge into the shallow river below. He tore out a few more of the loose stones from the wall and dropped them down. Then he rolled the big stone off the bridge. The trick was not to do too much, to let nature provide. A freak accident in the park, the police were bound to conclude. A woman jogger trips, then falls from the old stone bridge, and she's crushed by a small avalanche of stones falling into the river. He'd checked; there had been accidental deaths on these paths before. He had done the first part of what needed to be done. His associate could go to court and do the rest.

CHAPTER TWO

In my mind, I could still see my friend Jerry's wife dressed for burial, though the funeral was a week past. Karen had looked pretty, even in the coffin, her curly brown hair and small features perfectly composed. But I knew her husband had seen only a stranger in the fine wood box. The living don't resemble the dead.

I had been to four funerals over the past few years, but this was the first one where all I felt was sad. The other deaths were people who got in someone's way, who had been killed for greed. I was angry at their funerals. But Karen hadn't been murdered. There was no one to go after, no ready way to turn grief into a fight. She'd died young of cancer, nothing else. It was a while since I'd witnessed an ordinary death.

The minister's words had to do with spring and the renewal of life. Spring had always meant renewal to me, too. I'd played minor-league baseball twenty years before. Third base. I still had a habit of looking forward to the new season no matter what kind of year I had. Now even baseball had lost much of its appeal.

Today, on a Saturday afternoon in April, I was in the park alone. On spring weekends this year, Jerry and I had worked together carving wood from a large maple brought down by a late-winter storm. We made benches, new resting places for the wooded parts of the park, volunteer work for the Chestnut Hill Community Association. Soothing labor, he called it. Jerry said building the benches had helped him make it through Karen's illness and death. In my case, I liked the work because it was a good balance to the rest of my life, when I tried to cage corrupt little gods.

Jerry and I were friends even though Karen and I had been lovers before they met, and he knew that. She was as close as I've ever come to getting a relationship right. For all that, we lasted five months. She loved me, she said, but hated the risks I took. Hate beat love. After me, she found Jerry. He was safe. I eventually got to like the fact she had him. He was a very good guy. I used to take some comfort in how they lived. They'd had more than a decade of decent married years, as far as I could tell. These days, that made them pretty rare. I had envied the way they made it work, especially since I always found a way to end up alone. But there was more than one path to solitude.

I was finishing carving one of the benches by myself. I worked the maple into shape, pulling slabs of clean white wood out of the heart of the tree. A bench was simple work. The park trustees wanted it to look rustic so I didn't smooth the ends and I left bark on the thick round legs. I was hammering nails when Jerry came by. Seeing him in jeans again helped erase the image of him in a black mourner's suit by her graveside.

He didn't say hello. He sat down near me. He was a big guy with an easy look, blond hair, and a round face. During the week he managed a furniture store, a place I liked. He took out his hammer and let it rest in his hand. His eyes were dark and wide, his face lined from missed nights of sleep and the worries that went along with the grief.

He glanced at the bench. "Nice work, Gray."

"Goes easier with two," I said. "How are things at home?"

"I took the week off from work to be with the kids." He had three. "Karen's mother comes over a lot. She's there now. But she's also got a job herself." He shook his head, struck by some thought. "We make quite a pair. We get along, but it's like we're stuck with each other, without Karen." He got up. "I was just walking. Thought I'd come by. I've got to get back home."

I got up, piled the leftover wood, and packed away my tools.

"Come on. I'll go back with you if you like."

"That'd be good," he said.

We walked out of the park, past the spot on the road where he normally parked. He hadn't brought his car. It was three miles to his place. I suggested we go by my house and get my car, but he wanted to walk. I didn't mind. Chestnut Hill was beautiful anytime. In the spring, the back roads were full of blossoming trees.

"Even though you stopped the guy, that damn sign's still there," Jerry said, as we turned the corner onto Bell's Mill Road.

I didn't have to look to know what he meant. We were walking past one of the largest undeveloped chunks of land in Philadelphia outside of Fairmount Park, fifty acres of pasture and trees. A white sign planted firmly in the grass by the road read FUTURE SITE OF LUXURY CONDOMINIUMS—HOUGHTON PROPERTIES INC. Signs like that are usually followed by big tractors pulling up grassy chunks and uprooting old trees. Not this time.

"They really loved that land," Jerry said, sounding sad, as if the land were another thing that had died.

We knew the people who'd owned that particular piece of Chestnut Hill. They'd lived in a small house on the far end of the property for over fifty years and had left the land otherwise untouched all that time.

"Yeah, but love wasn't enough to protect it," I said. The old man had died first, two years ago, and his wife had died last year. Her will left the land to the city, to keep or sell as it wished, but with one condition: The land was supposed to remain undeveloped, to be used as open space. Everyone in the area knew about this land.

"I wish he'd take those signs down," Jerry said.

"That's out of my control," I answered. "It's private property. He can keep the signs up as long as he wants. But the land won't be touched."

Despite the restriction in the old woman's will, a developer had managed to buy the land, and then the sign went up.

It wasn't in my nature to leave that kind of puzzle alone. I went to City Hall, and I took Jerry with me because he was curious. We found answers in real estate deeds, zoning records, and building permit files. The records were public. Anyone could look, but people rarely did. I'd made a career out of records like that. It took one day's work to find the developer's clever manipulation of the terms of the old folks' will. He had hired an intermediary to buy the land first, complete with the required legal limitation. The developer then bought the land from the intermediary, but the intermediary conveniently failed to pass along the will's restriction to the developer.

I stopped the developer by threatening to take evidence to the DA. His scheme was a violation of state law. When he agreed to leave the land alone, I agreed to leave him alone. I'd been doing battle with people like him for years. I went from being a minor-league ballplayer to a sportswriter. And then I became a real newspaper reporter. But my ethics—or lack of them—lost me that job. It didn't bother me much anymore that blackmail was the method I had used against guys like the developer. I called them little gods because people like him made their own rules and did whatever they wanted to do. They always left victims behind. I could stop them by gathering evidence on their schemes and threatening to turn them in. To avoid the risk of going to jail, they curbed their scams, paid back their victims, and gave me a cut as well. I had developed an odd line of work, but there was always enough business.

We soon got to Roxborough, where Jerry lived. It was a tree-lined working-class section of the city where the houses were mostly brick Colonials, fairly inexpensive, and where every other neighbor was a cop. Most of the houses on his block had one or two kids out front, patrolling the cracked sidewalks on bikes or playing ball. If a house happened to have no kids outside at the moment, signs of their presence were evident. In Jerry's front yard, a basketball lay unattended on the grass and a bike was leaned upright against a big tree.

Jerry stopped me before I could say goodbye.

"I've got a problem you could help me with. The way you found out about the developer and that land . . . maybe you can do something for me."

"Of course," I said instantly, not knowing what the problem might be. I had wondered why he had pointed out the sign. It wasn't a novelty anymore. We passed it all the time. Now I understood: He'd been thinking about scams. Maybe there was more bad news, although nothing could be as bad as Karen's death.

There was a holiday decoration on the door, silk flowers and paper bunnies, though Easter was three weeks past. Karen had probably left it behind. Jerry stood there and didn't go in. Coming home must be hard for him these days, every single time, I thought.

His younger son, Kyle, who was six, came running up. The other boy, Sean, was fifteen. I knew the kids on sight but that was about all. Jerry patted his son on the shoulder, while the small boy looked at me with a sullen face.

"Where's Sean?" Jerry asked him.

"Grandma sent him to the store for milk."

Jerry nodded. He turned to me. "No sound from the little one. I guess she's asleep upstairs. Would you believe she's eighteen months old already?"

We went inside and sat down in the living room. Kyle disappeared, and a minute later I heard the distinctive sound of a video game in the basement.

"Karen's mom's upstairs with the baby," Jerry said. "She just sits there while the baby sleeps." He looked at the stairs. "You want anything to drink?"

I said no and he settled back on the couch.

"So what's it all about?" I asked him.

"Karen's life insurance," he said. "We had a policy. And now she's gone and the insurance agent tells me we aren't getting what we thought we would."

He glanced at me to see what I thought. I didn't think anything yet. He went on.

"Karen always kept the records and paid the bills. I didn't even think about insurance until someone asked me whether we had a policy. I knew we had insurance, and that's when I realized I had to call the insurance agent."

"When did you find out something was wrong?"

"I found everything in the desk." He pointed across the

room to a wooden cabinet. "The file she kept was pretty complete. The name of the agent, the agency, the company—they were right on top. I called the agent. He was decent on the phone. Didn't give me any kind of hard time. We talked awhile and then he asked me for numbers from the papers. Told me to send him the death certificate, and in return I'd be getting a check for the full amount, two hundred fifty thousand. He'd put a rush on it because—and I remember him saying this one thing—he knew how important it was for me to have the money."

"And then?"

"He called me back a few days later and said there was a problem. He showed up here to talk. He said Karen had left out information when we applied for the policy. There were medical conditions she hadn't put on the form, and because of that, we weren't going to get the money. He had this tone, like the thing he was telling me was embarrassing, like Karen had lied to me or had some secret past. Which made me nuts. If she didn't tell me things from her past, I don't hold that against her. The guy made it sound like we had something to be ashamed of."

"What did he say was left out?"

Jerry grimaced. "You know Karen died of ovarian cancer, right? Well, the agent said she'd been treated a couple of times before she met me for sexually transmitted diseases. And those diseases, if you have them often enough, can lead to pelvic something-or-other. It had initials. And he said she had that, too, which can lead to ovarian cancer. He said the insurance company was entitled to that information when we filled out the application. And because they didn't get it, they don't have to pay."

"Did he have documents, show you records of Karen's earlier medical problems?"

"Yeah. He had a whole file. Records from hospitals, financial papers, the whole thing."

"Did he leave you copies?"

He shook his head no. "I called a lawyer. One of the ones that advertises on TV. I told him what I told you. He said that the insurance agent was right. If the application information isn't complete, like medical history, you don't get the money. That's the way it works. He advised me to negotiate with him for a smaller sum. But I know one thing: Karen wouldn't have lied on that form, or to me, about something as important as this, no matter what they say."

He knew Karen better than I did, but we'd both loved her. I couldn't picture her lying for money. We looked at each other. He didn't like leaving these questions unanswered. I didn't either. And I could do something about it. I had a way.

CHAPTER THREE

No one was home when Jim Hartman drove up to Joan Moller's place. That was good. A string of morning meetings hadn't left him much time to prepare. He could take a few minutes to review a file he'd put together about the family. It was also better to meet her outside of her house, when she wasn't expecting his visit. The woman was grieving for her husband. Any further discomfort Hartman could add to her pain could only aid his plan.

He grabbed his briefcase, then walked the few steps to Mrs. Moller's house. He sat down on the steps of the red-brick two-story row house in the working-class Mayfair section of Philadelphia, glancing up the block now and then when he sensed someone coming. He'd only met Mrs. Moller once, years ago, and had no recollection of her appearance. But he had an impression of her nonetheless, pieced together from the details in the file and the way she sounded on the phone.

She was thirty-seven, had once worked as a nurse, and for the past five years had stayed home with her two young children. There were no relatives in the area, and nothing had ever been easy for her. Both of the children were in school and now, a month after her husband's death, and in the middle of the day, she would surely be worried, worn out, and very alone.

Mr. Moller had died of a heart attack at age forty, an unusual occurrence among the unscreened young population who typically bought insurance policies from Hartman. The young were the closest thing to a sure bet; they rarely got seriously ill or died. But the policy Hartman had sold the Mollers made a sure bet even better. They'd never get a payoff from the insurance company because they didn't actually have a policy; they only thought they did.

He sold legitimate life insurance policies as well, but his sale to the Mollers was part of a lucrative sideline in fraudulent insurance. In these cases, he sent in the initial premium payments to one of the country's largest insurance companies, starting a legitimate policy, obtaining official documents for clients to tuck in a drawer as proof they were covered. But soon after, Hartman began to pocket the monthly premium payments, never sending the insurance company another dime.

What made the scheme so sweet was that clients sent their payments to him, and Hartman ran his own branch office. Companies notified agents, not customers, when policies were canceled for nonpayment. It simply never occurred to anyone in the corporation that the agent might keep the monthly payments or fail to pass along word of a cancellation. Insurance was the perfect business for fraud. People paid money for years for something essentially invisible, a product they never expected to use until they died.

For thirteen years, the Mollers had sent Jim Hartman a check every month for $175. They believed they had purchased security; if one of them died, a substantial sum of money was due the one left behind.

Their relationship with the agency, and the potential payoff from the company in case of death, was a matter of trust. It was also a matter of contract. They had bought something concrete and paid for it on the installment plan. It was a sensible thing to do, most people thought. You might end up making only a few payments before your family got a big windfall. All that was needed was for one of you to die. Mr. Moller had done his part. Now his wife wanted payment. And it was time for Hartman to put his endgame into action.

From his vantage point on the stone steps, he watched people pass. He'd grown up with working-class people like this. He understood them. To find ways to take their money, it helped to understand them. He'd always had an easy way with other people's points of view, a knack for fitting in when that's what he wanted to do.

The main thing he understood about ordinary people was their fatigue. They worked two jobs. They worried about the work, whether it would last, and whether they could cover their bills until the next paycheck. It wasn't only the labor that was tiring. It was the worrying itself, it was all the evidence in their lives that they had failed—as parents and spouses and workers. They were pushovers for kind words and a little hope.

But this woman had been tough, starting when she notified him of her husband's death. He told her then about a surprising aspect of their policy, previously ignored, newly clarified, critically affecting the equity. She wouldn't receive the expected amount. His experience was that when the explanation was good—and his explanations were very well crafted—the survivors eventually accepted the lie and the smaller sum he offered. But this particular widow refused.

He had gone through his usual routines, but she wasn't defeated by his string of useless answers, his intentionally wearying phone calls, one after another. From each conversation she gleaned some bit of information and built around it like an oyster making a pearl, each question leading her to call him again. Eventually she called the insurance company whose name was on the canceled policy—Bethlehem Casualty & Life. Very few of his clients went that far. Even when they did, he was prepared.

A representative at Bethlehem Casualty accurately informed her that her husband's policy had lapsed and told her to call her agent. So back to Hartman she came. That was no problem for him, though it might become one if she persisted. She needed persuading that the problem was not in the policy but in her family and herself.

A woman came down the block, and the age and look of her was right. He stirred himself from the steps. She had black hair, streaming loose down the back of her blue jacket. Her skin was pale, whether the effect of her grief or the result of days spent out of the sun. He got up, eager to greet her.

"Joan Moller?"

The woman stopped walking. She held herself stiffly, arms tight at her sides, a bag heavy with groceries in each hand. She had slight white lines on the soft insides of her palms from the pressure of the thin handles.

"Yes, what is it?" She seemed startled, as if anyone wanting anything of her was a surprise.

Hartman introduced himself and reminded her they'd talked by phone.

"I didn't realize you'd come." She rested the bags on the steps. "I hoped you'd find the mistake, whatever it was, and just send a check."

"I'm here to explain about that," he said. "We need to talk."

"I'm very upset the benefit wasn't paid. I'm going to have to see a lawyer and make a real fuss."

"Can I help you with those?" He pointed to the bags, ignoring her confrontational tone.

"I can do it." She started up the short flight of steps.

He picked up his briefcase and followed. "I have some paperwork to show you."

She didn't answer but unlocked the door and let him follow her in. It was a small house. The entryway was narrow, the living room crammed with furniture. The kitchen had a small alcove that also served as a dining room and foyer. She went straight to the kitchen table to put down the bags. The house was neat. He had visited many widows over the years. Most of them kept the physical parts of their lives in as much order as they could.

She sat at the kitchen table. "Show me your papers," she said, her voice firm.

"As I told you on the phone," Hartman said, "there's very little money in the policy. I know you're upset about that. That's why I wanted to visit, to explain personally."

The woman looked at him blankly. "The policy was for two hundred thousand dollars. What kind of explanation could there be?"

"There is one," he said, "but you'll find it hard to hear."

She didn't say anything. That was good.

"There's a reason the policy has almost no money in it, despite the premiums you've paid the past thirteen years. Two years ago your husband came to our agency and arranged for a loan."

The more matter-of-fact the better, he reminded himself. He spoke slowly.

"Your husband eventually borrowed the entire balance as it

stood at that time, about twenty-five thousand dollars. After that, he came back twice—whenever the equity built up again—and took out additional, smaller loans. Because the equity was almost gone, there was very little money left for a payout in the event of his death."

"That can't be," the woman said. She leaned forward, one hand across her lips. "My husband would never have done that without telling me. There's no way."

"It's hard to accept, I know," Hartman said, "but it's absolutely true."

"That's ridiculous," she said, angry now. "You're saying my husband withdrew all the money from the policy? Why would he do that? And without telling me."

Hartman leaned toward her, his face close to hers. He kept his voice low. "In my line of work, I see people deceive each other all the time, especially men and their wives. Finding out about it hurts. Maybe it makes people stronger in the end. I don't know."

He shook his head and watched her react. He tried to read her expression. Perhaps she was thinking about her husband, the inevitable hurtful memories, small betrayals; the things he had really done and the things she knew he was capable of doing, simply because he was a man.

"I can tell you more about what your husband did, if you want me to," Hartman said gently. "It's our business to find out, when tragedies like this occur."

"I still don't know what you're talking about," she said.

"At this point, there's a total of only fifteen hundred dollars' worth of equity in the policy. That's the money you're due, the payment we referred to when we talked on the phone. I'm upset about what's happened to you, Joan." His tone was non-committal, matter-of-fact, the accountant dispassionately delivering bad financial news.

"The policy was for two hundred thousand dollars," she said, insistent again.

Now it was time to convince her to surrender all expectations for being paid. To do the job, the story had to hurt. Each set of lies was different. The construction required a talent for understanding what caused people pain.

"The loans aren't all of it," Hartman said. "Your husband had another life. We use investigators in these situations to get the full picture, so we can help the survivors understand what's occurred. Otherwise they blame us, and it's really not our fault. The report we got indicates your husband was a regular week-day player at the Atlantic City casinos. Weren't there days off and evenings he worked late, nights he told you he was doing things with friends?"

They were foolproof questions; the only possible answer was yes. He watched the woman think about those nights for a minute, then went on.

"It looks like your husband spent substantial time in those places. The money he took from the policy was his stake."

"No, no." She looked away. "He couldn't have done that." Her voice was a whisper. "He wasn't even interested in gambling."

"It wasn't just gambling." He made himself sound reluctant, as if it was hard to continue. "When a man spends twenty-five thousand dollars at a casino, the place provides comforts, food and drinks and a place to stay. But women are a part of what they provide. Your husband took advantage of that, too."

"I don't believe you." Her voice was weak. "But even if it happened—these things—I still have the policy. If I get all of the money from the policy, I can pay back what Brian took."

He noticed the way she phrased it.

"I'm afraid not. The way it works is if you take out a loan, the policy's not in effect until the loan's paid back. That's the way it works. Otherwise everyone would borrow as much as they could all the time, knowing their family could still collect when the family member died. You can see the problem with that, can't you? The insurance companies would never have any money."

There was a little more to say.

"Even if the policy was still in effect, your husband was in such debt to the casinos that the two hundred thousand dollars wouldn't go to you, but to them. He liked to gamble but he wasn't good at it. Joan, at the time of his death, he owed the casinos more than the policy was worth."

She didn't say anything else.

"I can't help but believe that knowing what he'd done, the shame might have contributed to his death of a heart attack so young."

He watched his words make their impact. She stood up suddenly, the chair sliding back behind her until it hit the wall. She backed up farther, as if retreating from the words. The seat of the chair caught the back of her knees and caused her to sit down again. The motion was odd and she almost fell. She leaned forward, bearing the weight of what she had heard, her face sunk deep into the dark curve of her palms. Tears pressed out from between her fingers and ran down the back of her wrists, while she turned her head away.

He got up, reached into his briefcase, took out the check for fifteen hundred dollars, and put it on the kitchen table. He let himself out. It had taken fifteen or twenty minutes, no more. But it wasn't necessarily over. That depended on the widow. She might pick herself up and come after him again. If she did, she'd have to die.

CHAPTER FOUR

Morning was the slowest time in the week at A.M. papers like *The Philadelphia Inquirer.* The energy started building in late afternoon, and rolled heavier and heavier until the first-edition deadline at nine in the evening. Mornings were downtimes, and most reporters came strolling in at noon.

I didn't even try to pull into the *Inquirer* parking lot; that was out of the question. Competition for those slots was like trying to get tickets for the Super Bowl. Reporters waited years, and then still had to kill to get a spot. I had no parking pass. But I lucked out and got a meter right across from the small commercial lot next to Westy's Bar. I decided to use the back door. Nothing had changed. The sign on the facade said VISITORS MUST USE BROAD STREET ENTRANCE. I might not work for a newspaper anymore, but I had stopped feeling like a visitor a long time ago. I strolled right in.

The guard in the booth didn't stir when I went by. I knew if he hadn't recognized me, he would have stopped me cold. He did his job in the simplest possible way. You either passed by while he played statue or you didn't get in. I was pretty sure he had no idea what it was, exactly, most of the fifteen hundred people in the building did. What mattered was whether he knew your face. I didn't go in very often. Maybe it was some kind of newspaper look that I had retained.

Whatever the look was, I'd had it all my life. My ex-wife used to say my looks were good lies. She was an expert on men's looks, so I knew she was right. What she meant was that my thick crop of light-brown hair and a face that aged slow made me look younger than thirty-eight. I was six-two and built pretty big, but I looked smaller because most of me was thin. Somewhere around the chest and shoulders I started to expand; as a result I had legs built for speed and a top like a block. Long after sports had stopped being the biggest part of my life, I still worked out as if I were getting paid for the effort. It was easy to stay motivated. I had a vision: to acquire some smarts by getting older without losing all of my strength. It was a veteran's approach to the game.

I walked up to the business-news department on the fourth floor. All newsrooms look the same: big, wide, open spaces, desks scattered everywhere. And most of all, no walls. Nothing separates you from anyone else. The most communal workplace there is, other than a factory floor, is a newspaper. It is a working community of which I was no longer a part. I was feeling something more than nostalgia. It was sight-seeing from beyond the grave. When you have had a profession and given it up, something personal is always lost. I had been a reporter for only two years. But every time I walked into a newsroom, I got homesick.

I was there to do research, to find out how the insurance industry worked. Reporters become experts one story at a time; what you end up knowing depends on the stories you do. Insurance had never been an area I'd covered. I knew a business reporter at the *Inquirer* named Tyler who'd become an expert in many areas over the years. I thought insurance was likely to be one of them. Seeing Tyler was a quick way to get the background I needed. I'd tried calling him earlier but only got his voice mail. He could have been two feet away or in another country. I decided to visit. If he wasn't around, I'd find another business reporter who could help.

I headed for Tyler's office at the back of the business newsroom. Offices were usually reserved for editors and administrative types, rarely for reporters. Tyler was a reporter, but he had earned an office because of the way he worked and how productive he had been. His stories were crystal-clear. His office was a famous mess. He worked at two desks, back-to-back, the surfaces of both completely covered with papers, the wall across from them a set of floor-to-ceiling bookshelves. They were filled with his files, old black loose-leaf folders containing detailed compilations, numbers and words, nothing but facts.

His specialty was creating painstaking descriptions of the economic reality of how America actually worked. It was a reality few people wanted to know, yet one of great worth. The clutter of his office stood in clear contrast to the clean and simple language of his stories, his dispassionately detailed accounts of how the rich always got richer and the rest of us paid the price. I'd admired him for a long time. But none of Tyler's truths had ever changed the world's ways.

A few feet outside Tyler's office was a reporter hunched over her desk, staring into a computer terminal's green glow. She was talking into the air, asking questions aloud and apparently hearing answers out of the surrounding silence, as if in conversation with ghosts. She had on a reporter's telephone headset, lightweight and compact. I glanced back at the length of the newsroom. There were a half-dozen people in similar conversations, questioning oracles, marking the answers on fields of green light.

I walked in through the open door of Tyler's office. His famil-

iar things were there but he wasn't. I looked down through the
tall window at Broad Street, where taxis and pedestrians played
chicken. If Tyler wasn't around, I'd have to work a little harder.
Most reporters knew I used to be a reporter and now did private investigations. Some had a problem with that. Others, like
Tyler, used their instincts to decide whom to like. I would have
told him everything if he had asked me, but he never did.

"Gray?" Saying my name was his greeting. "To what do I
owe the pleasure?"

I turned to see the man I was looking for. He was short,
bald, and pudgy. He had a friendly voice. The body wasn't a
threat to anyone, but the brain inside it was. He'd done a lot of
good damage over the years.

"You know," I said.

It wasn't like we'd ever had dinner. He wasn't that kind of
friend. But he liked the kind of enemies I made, and he liked
helping me make them. He never made me do any kind of
dance for information. He sat down in the armchair, lay back,
put his feet up on the desk, stretched his arms up behind his
head. This was a man who enjoyed knowing things.

"Fire away," Tyler said.

"Okay. I need some background about the insurance industry. It's a business I've never really understood."

"That's pretty normal. Most people don't understand insurance. And the insurance people obviously like it that way."

"Tell me about it," I said, as I grabbed a chair and sat.

"Insurance is an interesting business from a reporter's point
of view. Because it's very big, and very hard to see. By big, I
mean the insurance industry is one of the most profitable businesses in the world." He paused for a second, closed his eyes as
if pulling together a batch of his files, then went on.

"Together, all the insurance companies gross over a hundred billion dollars a year. And there isn't a bit of federal regulation. You compare that to banking or securities or anything else. A bank has to tell you the exact interest rate it offers for saving or borrowing. But insurance companies only give you an estimate of what your return might be. And since what they say is never reviewed by anyone in federal government, or covered by federal laws, they just lie, tell you you're getting returns you don't really get. On Wall Street, the SEC lets a lot get by, but at least they're there. The insurance industry rides completely high and free."

"What else do they get away with?" I asked.

"The key to their big profits is the fact that their customers don't understand how insurance works. There are two basic kinds of life insurance. One kind is what's called whole life, known also by other names—universal life, investment insurance, insurance savings plans, and other words like that. The other kind is called term. Ninety percent of all the insurance sold in America is the whole-life kind. And people should almost never have it. They should have term instead."

"I've heard of both kinds, but I don't really know the difference."

"You and almost everybody else. Term insurance is pretty simple and relatively cheap. You make monthly payments on the order of maybe ten to fifty dollars, depending on your age and your coverage. If you die during the term of your policy, your family gets a lump sum, say three or four hundred thousand dollars, whatever your monthly premium bought. That's all it is. You're betting you're going to die sooner rather than later, and if you do, your family gets paid. The insurance company bets you're going to live long enough for them to make a profit on the monthly payments you make, and the investment income they get from that money. Neither you nor your family ever gets a penny back unless you die.

"Most people give up their insurance after they retire and the kids are grown," he continued, "so the insurance companies rarely have to pay. It's a good game for them. But also a decent deal for the individual buyer. It's a reasonable risk, for relatively low prices. If insurance companies sold only term, they'd make a great profit and basically be an honest industry."

"But mostly they sell the other kind, whole life," I said.

"Right. And they don't just offer it or sell it—nothing as mild as that. They desperately push it, do anything to get someone to buy it, because it's the main source of their profit. Whole life costs ten times as much as term for the same payout.

"The pitch they give you is that a whole-life policy is like a savings plan. Save for the kids' college tuition, save for retirement, on and on. It's better than term life, they tell you, because you get all your money back in the end, not only the death benefit but also all the cash you put in. Plus, even before anyone dies, you can borrow against the equity in your policy."

"That is a good pitch," I said.

"Sure, but there's a ton they don't tell you. They don't tell you that for the first ten years of a whole-life policy you have almost no equity, and you can only borrow very small amounts or nothing at all. That's supposedly because during the first ten years they're investing the money for you, so it's not available for your use. After that, their fortune in hand, they let your equity start to build. But you really don't know the rate of interest you're getting, because either they don't reveal it or their explanations are unintelligible or outright lies. You'd almost always do better if you'd simply put your monthly premium payments in a savings bank, or a CD, or a money market fund, or invest them in stocks or mutual funds. In fact, there's no way, given the full story, most people would ever put a dime in whole life."

I told him exactly what Jerry's problem was and asked him what he thought.

"That's a new one on me," he said. "Just outright not paying a death benefit? I don't see how even they could get away with that. But what the agent's saying doesn't really sound all that wild. If someone did leave important information off their application, the company would have a legitimate case that they were misled. I mean, I don't trust insurance companies or their agents, but are you sure the insurance company is lying?"

I knew what I felt about Karen and about what Jerry said, but I needed to prove it. Maybe some of the background Tyler gave me could help.

"By the way," I said, "what did you mean before when you said the industry was 'hard to see'?"

"If you wanted to do a story about insurance, where would you go?" he replied. "There's almost nothing about insurance in public records. And although most states have an insurance commission—in our state they call it a department—the state doesn't have the legal power to obtain all the financial information or enforce rules. Besides, the insurance commissioners in most states are already in the pocket of the insurance industry—they're often people in the insurance business themselves. On the state level, it's a game. The commissions don't even have key information, because the insurance companies don't give it out and commissions don't ask for it; they don't want it. For example, auto insurance rates in Philadelphia are among the highest in the country. The insurance companies say that without high rates they'd lose money because there are so many fraudulent claims in the city. But no one knows exactly how much fraudulent claims total, or even how much the companies actually make. And none of that information is in public records. Almost nothing about insurance companies is."

"That's for the industry as a whole," I said. I was thinking about Jerry. "But if what I'm looking into is a specific company, there's got to be a way." I thought for a minute. "If it was a story about land, you'd look at real estate records, right?"

He nodded. "And if it was about a program funded by the city, you'd look at city contracts."

We went on running it down together, systematically and out loud. It was territory reporters knew well.

"Bankruptcy," I offered.

"Bankruptcy court," he said. "No problem."

"Hospitals?"

"Public audits. Department of Health records. Patient charts as a primary source. And lots of other things."

"Let's step back," I suggested. "What's life insurance basically about?"

"It depends how basic you want to get," he said. "At its simplest, insurance is about fear, I guess." He stopped for a minute. "All kinds of fear," he went on, "but mostly fear of death, I think."

"Agreed. And there are public records that deal with death."

"Sure. Death certificates, accident reports, mortality statistics."

"It's not just death, it's death and money," I said. "And there are public records that deal with just those two things." The place where wills are processed, I thought, where people go to seek the wealth that belonged to the dead. He looked at me, stuck, but it only lasted a second.

"Probate court," he said.

I had a place to start a search. I wondered if Tyler might want to get involved. It wasn't hard to see that what happened to Jerry might make a good story. But a reporter, no matter how good, wouldn't be able to get Jerry his money. And if he put the story in the paper, I'd have no tools for blackmail.

I was looking at him and wondering how to put it. "Look, Tyler, you might—"

He somehow spotted it coming before I finished.

"You don't have to worry. I'm knee-deep in a project on the IRS. I don't have time to follow your trail, even if I wanted to. Which I don't."

"Thanks," I said, getting up.

"Feel free to call again," he said, the way a storekeeper speaks to a departing customer. Tyler's free-facts store, construction materials for building truths. I had to do the rest myself.

"Maybe I will." I walked out of the office. The phone was ringing at the woman's desk. She picked up her headset. Half-way through the newsroom, I looked back and watched her staring at the screen, talking to the air.

CHAPTER FIVE

This time when I pulled up at Jerry's house there was no sign of the boys. The bicycle and basketball were tucked away and the kids were in school. Loved ones die, and to all appearances, as if nothing has happened, life goes on.

It wasn't one person that greeted me, but two. I'd forgotten about the third child. At that moment, she was resting comfortably in Jerry's thick arms. Her little form fit neatly. She was full of yawns and her eyes were half open. She had one small hand wrapped tight around one of Jerry's fingers. At that age, holding on was a big part of the day's work.

We sat down in the living room.

"I appreciate your looking into this for me," he said. "I feel like I ought to be able to handle it somehow, but I don't know what to do."

He sounded embarrassed about his situation, about being on the wrong end of things.

"It's okay," I said. "I think we can straighten this out. I did some research about insurance. I just need to ask some questions to start."

He nodded. "Go ahead."

"Okay. How much were your monthly premium payments for the life insurance?"

"About two hundred," Jerry said, "but part of it was savings. So no matter what else happens, we should still at least have that."

I took a deep breath and explained to him what I'd learned. The large premium amount they were paying meant their policy was the wrong kind—whole life. Karen had died after they'd paid into the policy for nine years. That meant, as Tyler explained it, they had almost nothing built up yet as savings—despite the twenty thousand they'd paid in.

"Believe it or not, they probably don't owe you any money in savings," I told him.

"All that money we put in every month," he said, incredulous, "we don't get any of it back?"

"That's right," I said. "And that's the legal part of how insurance companies do business. It's complicated. What we really need to get at is whether the insurance company did something illegal or wrong in not paying the death benefit, the two hundred fifty thousand dollars. That's what we're going after."

"Just tell me what to do," Jerry said.

"First, let me see the policy."

He got up, went into another room, and brought back the policy. It was on fancy paper, like parchment, and very long, like a scroll. It looked like the Declaration of Independence. At the top was the name of one of America's largest insurance companies: Bethlehem Casualty & Life. It had a multitude of numbers on it. Some of the numbers made sense, like the amount of the policy and the monthly schedule of payments. The rest looked as though they'd been thrown in for filler. Documents as confusing as this didn't get that way by accident. But confusing sales documents were normal in most of the business world and didn't mean this particular paperwork was bad.

I skipped to the bottom, because that's where the name I wanted would be. "James Hartman" was on the last line of the paper, a small, barely readable signature scrawled above the type. I pointed to the name.

"Is this the man you spoke to?"

"Yes," Jerry said. He had an accusing tone, as if Hartman were a mugger.

"Okay," I said. "I'll take this and photocopy it later. Here's what I want you to do."

I coached him then, giving him the quick course on how to talk to a con artist and still get what you want. It was a skill good reporters acquired. It consisted mostly of persistence. But it also helped to be single-minded, interested only in what you needed and nothing else. It would also help if Jerry seemed vulnerable, needy, and desperate for the information, not at all a threat. He had a good head start at looking that way.

"Here's how to do it. You go to Hartman's office, wait there to see him, wait all day if you have to. That's because you're desperate, you see?"

Jerry nodded.

"When you see him you're sad, in grief, sincere. You need his shoulder to lean on. You're not angry, you have nothing against him. You just need to see the file again, the one he showed you when he was here in your house, the one with Karen's medical records. You tell him you have to see it in cold black and white so you can finally get it out of your system, really believe it happened, that Karen kept that part of her past a secret from you."

I saw his jaw tighten, but he didn't say anything. It was hard for him already, and he hadn't even gone to Hartman's office yet.

"He'll change the subject, try to steer you in different directions," I continued. "Don't let him. That can be difficult—you'll see what I mean. But you just keep coming back to one point, saying you have to see that file. Understand?"

He nodded again, but I didn't trust his understanding. He was still in shock from losing his wife and dealing with thieves. There was a reasonable possibility he hadn't heard a word. I needed to check.

"So tell me what I said," I pushed him.

He didn't protest. Maybe he wasn't sure himself if he had it right. "Nothing matters but the file," he said. His voice was flat, but he had the key part right, so I went on.

"Eventually, I'm certain he'll show it to you. When you see it, remember to look at it like it means something to you. If you play it right, Hartman will act sympathetic. It won't hurt to ask him then if you can make a copy. What we need are the names of the hospitals or clinics where Karen was treated, the city or cities they were in, and the dates she was treated—at least the years. If you get the name of the health insurance company that covered her at the time, that would be good. If you can't get a copy—and he probably won't let you—at least memorize the hospital names."

The baby stirred and made some sounds that were not quite crying. He rocked her softly. I stopped and looked at him. He didn't wait for me to ask him to repeat what I had said.

"The hospitals, the city, the dates she was treated. The health insurance company, if I can. Right?"

The baby was louder. Jerry looked tired. I wanted to leave him alone. We had work to do, but the next move was his. I got up.

"Call me when you get the information," I said. "I can take over from there, and then we'll see if the insurance agent's story is true."

I knew he might not be able to do the job, that he might get too upset, or that Hartman might see through him and get spooked. But if this didn't work, we'd find something that would.

He went upstairs to try to put the baby down. I told him I'd wait. I called out when he was halfway up. He turned around.

"Is it okay if I look through your files down here? There might be something else we could use. I'd know."

"Do it," Jerry said. He and the babe in arms moved up and out of sight.

I toured the downstairs part of the house. I was searching for more than information for a case. I wanted to find something that would help to restore my own sense of security about how Karen had lived. I was looking for evidence of a life lived within normal frames, whatever that was. I walked into the den and over to the old wooden desk and began pawing through the accumulated records of the part of Karen and Jerry's life that was over. The desk had three deep drawers on each side and a long narrow one in the middle. I pulled them open one by one.

I was looking through records of their life, as well as a part of mine. Two of the drawers held piles of articles and newspaper clips, mostly about poverty and health. Karen had been a social worker. Drawers full of work-related articles were an occupational hazard. Social workers were like teachers, always saving stuff they might be able to use for their work. There were also some articles on how to care for the terminally ill. My guess was she clipped them before she got sick, to use to help someone else.

Bills and canceled checks were in another drawer, in neatly organized piles, this year, last year, and the year before. I picked up piles of checks and flipped through them. Every third one was to Caruso's or Top Shelf, the two best groceries in the area, or to the Flourtown farmers' market. My own pile of checks probably looked much the same. Jerry was an eater, big quantities, like me. Karen wouldn't have helped fatten that particular bill much, but they did have three kids.

I pulled open the third drawer. My vision suddenly blurred. It hurt. I knew immediately it was an item she'd saved, important to her, and therefore a token of loss. I picked it up and turned it over. It was a photograph. I recognized it immediately. She had held on to this particular piece of her life—not hers and Jerry's, but ours. Looking at it, I remembered the way we met, years ago.

I'd been looking into an agency called Hillside Community Services. It was a private, supposedly nonprofit company quickly created during the Great Society days of the sixties, one of the many that found a way to steal millions of federal dollars in the name of helping the poor.

I had been in Washington for several weeks, studying Hillside's federal contracts. The company took in twenty million a year but there was little evidence they helped anyone with the money. I went to their offices and pretended an interest in volunteer work. The routine for volunteers was to accompany social workers to the field. The woman in charge dialed two extensions before she found an available worker.

I remembered walking down the hall to Karen's office, seeing her for the first time. She had the room arranged so she sat with her back to the door. That meant when she turned around there wasn't anything between her and her visitors. It was a welcoming way to arrange things. She was pretty, and young enough to still be in college. She put her hands behind her neck and brushed back a lot of curly brown hair with her fingers. I hoped she wasn't part of the agency's schemes; staff often weren't. And I had already learned not to be surprised to find saints in bad places.

We took a ten-minute drive to an apartment building called Lasker House, a huge project for the poor, owned by Hillside. I'd read about the building in the records I'd researched. Hillside collected more than a million a year to manage the property and provide tenant services.

The people Karen was there to visit fell into one broad category: barely hanging on. They had a place to live because the government had made one available. The government had also given them some coverage for health care and food stamps. They didn't have much else. The building itself was in terrible condition. It was obvious from one quick look that the millions Hillside received hadn't been spent on improvements.

I accompanied Karen to the apartments and listened to the tenants' mild complaints. Whatever their situations, they rarely had much to say. One very old guy had a mantra he repeated to all her questions: "I been worse places than this." We heard rats in the dark corners. His faucets leaked and his stove didn't work. There were small holes in the plaster walls, metal stanchions visible under the stone wall.

He refused her advice to get help by complaining to government agencies. His body rarely changed position, set permanently slumped in his chair. But the hint of a smile crossed his thin, lined face, as if to let us know that figuring him out wasn't going to be easy. He wasn't depressed and he wasn't in any other conveniently labeled condition; it was something more than that. "I been worse places than this," he kept saying. I found myself wondering where else he'd been.

There was a young woman with three kids, two who never stopped talking and a smaller one who never spoke. The woman went to a training program in the morning, then picked the kids up from school and cared for them by herself all day and night.

Her oldest son had been caught stealing candy from a supermarket shelf. The shame was apparently so hard to bear she had stopped attending her program, and she had been avoiding Karen as well. She was staying home, Karen learned, to keep an eye on her son. What her boy's stealing meant was that she hadn't managed to protect him, hadn't managed to keep what went on at the Lasker House from seeping in through her closed door. It meant that what went on in the housing project had gotten to her son, despite the neat and orderly world she'd made of her small apartment.

There was a woman in her early seventies who asked Karen to get her into a nursing home. She wasn't ill enough or old enough to get admitted. But she was tired and scared of the way things were at the project. For her, life at Lasker was so bad that she preferred to go to a place where people spent most of their time praying to die.

Karen did what she could. She listened. Sometimes she helped them figure out how to deal with a problem. She didn't treat the tenants as ill or incapable, unless they really were. She took things one problem at a time. She didn't get lost in the helplessness that comes from lumping all problems together. Hardest of all, she kept herself out of it. There was no ego. It wasn't about whether she looked good or was good, or whether they knew it or did what she said. She didn't get angry at them or herself when the problems remained or got worse. She did what she could and moved on. I imagined the tenants were better off for talking to her. But she could offer little in the way of substantial solutions. The problems were too much of a burden for her skills alone.

What I learned from the visit was that the Lasker project was destitute despite the millions the federal government poured in. The only visible help tenants got from Hillside Community Services was the social workers' visits.

We made several trips like that. On our way back to the agency, Karen always drove like a maniac, taking every curve much too fast. I thought of her as fearless rather than reckless, probably just because I liked her. I wondered what else she did that wildly. I once suggested a deviation in our route.

"There's a place near here we ought to stop, if you like," I said. "Someplace pretty. I haven't been to it in a long time."

"Someplace pretty here? Well, why not," she said.

I pointed to the right. She drove the few blocks, then pulled over and stopped. We got out and she walked beside me, down the lane. We were in a section called Germantown, a neighborhood peculiar to Philadelphia: poor and interracial, but with beautiful old stone houses and laced with trees and open woods.

On the right side of us, a low-slung fence of pale raw wood framed part of the block. Rising up over it, dwarfing the simple design, was one after another of Germantown's imposing homes. At the end of the row of houses, trees took over the land. We walked down a slight hill. To the side was a little waterfall, the soft spray cutting across the rocks, pooling up in nooks and shelves of stone along the hill, then breaking through the little barriers, streaming past the dirt path.

I took her by the arm and gently pulled her toward me as she was about to step into the water and mud, unaware of the change in the ground. She let me steer her. I noticed she was looking at me and not the landscape. She turned toward me and came into my arms. All I did was stand still. It felt as if I already had everything I wanted. Then we kissed.

It is the most perfect memory I have. I remember the sky,

which was blue and as clear as skies get. I remember the look of the woods, the sharp, piercing glare of the light between the trees, the sound of water slipping over pebbles.

In a way, we never let go of each other after that, not until we had to. We spent every possible moment together. That one time, and never again, I put the victims second, set aside who I was and what I did. She did the same. She took days off for the first time in a year. Our coming together was intense, shared, and right. We both saw the way our meeting was going to change the rest of our lives.

Standing in Jerry's house, by the old desk, I held the photo of the waterfall in my hand; it was black and white, and fifteen years old. I wondered why she'd saved it.

I turned around and saw Jerry's oldest kid, Sean, in the hallway. He was staring at me. I didn't know how long he'd been there. He hadn't done anything to announce himself, but he wasn't hiding either. Even though I had his dad's permission, I was still an intruder, in so many ways. And he had the greater portion of grief.

"What the hell are you doing?" Sean said. "Where's my dad?"

"Upstairs," I said.

"Does he know you're snooping around down here?"

"Yeah, he does. I'm looking through your mom's things because I'm trying to help your dad, and you."

The boy walked past me into the living room. He sat on the couch, put his feet up on the coffee table, and opened the paper. I didn't think he was interested in sitting or reading. It was a territorial statement, I thought, his way of telling me that although I was there, the place was his.

I put the picture back where it had been and closed the drawer. Jerry came down the stairs. I said goodbye, but as I headed out, I glanced back and saw the boy get up from the couch and move toward the desk. He wanted to know what I had found. It was his right to see.

CHAPTER SIX

Jim Hartman drove to Center City and parked a half mile from the Mercer–Markwell Tower. It was the nighttime workplace of the woman he intended to kill. He had been there a number of times to prepare. It was a quarter to five in the afternoon. Hundreds of people were coming and going. Even at night, security was poor. By day, it was virtually nonexistent.

He walked into the crowded lobby and passed the guard station, then made his way up to the place he would wait—an unused and unfurnished office on the twenty-sixth floor. He had a key he'd stolen a few days ago. The office was small, only three empty rooms. He left the lights off and moved around as little as possible. He made himself comfortable, stretched out on the floor. He had three hours to wait.

The previous killings had been made to look like accidents; that was the point. On average, he arranged one wrongful-death case a year. But he could never be certain that the family would file a suit or choose the lawyer he wanted for them. So he usually picked two victims for potential litigation, to increase the odds. The lawyer's share of the verdict in these cases was quite often over a million. Hartman's cuts had already made him rich. But he wasn't in the business for the money. What he really loved was finding angles, making plans, and watching them work. So tonight he was trying something new. The family of this victim was going to be able to sue the building's owners for negligence, because lax security had gotten her killed.

At eight-thirty, he put on his jacket and coat and a pair of thin leather gloves. He carefully exited the office, making sure there was no one in the hall. He took the stairs down one flight. The Wheeler and Wilkins door was wood, framed in metal, with two thick clear-glass panels. There was no sign of the woman inside, but most of the office lights were on. He had always been thorough in scouting the killing ground; he had no doubt about the presence of his prey.

The victim had been carefully selected, as all of them were. Tracy Lucas was twenty-eight, a CPA, in her second year as an associate for Wheeler and Wilkins, which occupied the twenty-fifth floor. Hartman knew her parents from his neighborhood; they owned a small clothing store and had been his clients for years. They trusted him. He would comfort them in their grief; that meant he'd be in a good position to lead them to a lawyer.

Their only daughter was an independent type. She'd been living on her own since college, working hard to move up in a good job. He had heard much about her from her parents over the years, but she and Hartman had never even met. He knew, though, that she plied her skilled trade on a late shift, by herself. And most of the building was empty at that time. She was a perfect choice.

He took hold of the doorknob with one hand and put his body hard and tight against the frame. He eased up a bit, then pressed forward again, using his shoulder, bracing himself with his legs. There was a splintering, metallic sound as the lock tore out of its frame, then he was in. He closed the door behind him. He looked down the corridor at an alarmed Tracy Lucas, drawn to the noise.

"What do you want?" the woman said, the pitch of her voice made higher by fear.

"Tracy Lucas?"

"Yes," the woman answered. "Who are you?"

He moved toward her. There was a phone on the reception desk and she reached for it. He closed the distance, grabbed her wrist, and used it to turn her around. He gathered her long, thick brown hair in his hand and made a fist. He yanked her head back.

"I won't hurt you," he said to calm her.

Fear held her still and silent as much as his grip. She was pretty, her skin pale and freckled, brown hair a neat frame for her face. Her clothes were proper, a knee-length skirt, not tight, and the pale, smooth skin of her legs was given a sheen by the stockings. Hartman had time to look her over. Nice, he thought, distracted from his business for a second. But that would have been for another time and place.

He lifted his hands and tightened his gloves. He punched her in the mouth. A spurt of blood covered the bottom of her face and dripped down onto her chest. She fell back against the desk. She roused herself and struggled. Another punch flattened her nose and broke her teeth. Then she took a blow to the belly, and that stopped her breath. The beating was required for the plan. For a while, the sounds of the blows were louder than the noises the woman made. Then there was only the sound of the blows.

He grabbed the hem of her skirt in one hand and yanked it up, exposing her thighs. He noticed her underwear, pink pastel flowers on white cloth. He grabbed the sides of her shirt and ripped it off. The thin cotton split and tore; a button shot off and rolled across the floor. Almost naked now, she seemed very young.

He checked to make sure she'd stopped breathing. Then he stepped back and took in the scene he had created. If it worked, her family would make more money from the lawsuit than she ever could have made for them by her work.

He wiped his gloved hands off on the ripped blouse and skirt, then pulled out a pocket watch and checked the time. Only fifteen minutes had passed. These things never take long, he thought. What happened after would take years.

To kill someone and get away with it, it was important to understand the thinking of everyone who might become involved—most important, the police. If there was no obvious starting point in searching for her killer, a wide-open investigation could conceivably lead back to him. The solution was to have ready suspects for the detectives. This he was happy to do. In fact, no one he knew could do it better.

The first suspect was gift-wrapped. Hartman knew the woman had once had a boyfriend who roughed her up. Her parents had noticed bruises on her legs and marks on her shoulders after she'd been out. Even without their urging, she'd been strong enough to end it with the guy. They'd all been worried he might stick around, but that didn't happen. Now he was going to get a chance to be a prime suspect in his ex-girlfriend's murder. Hartman didn't have to do anything. The police would definitely ask the parents if she had had any enemies, past or present, and the parents would quickly provide the boyfriend's name.

But one suspect wasn't enough. So he used his computer, and because he was an insurance agent and needed to evaluate bids, he was able to obtain from the building's management a list of all employees working in this commercial tower. He cross-checked that list against the criminal court information fully available to the public on the Internet. Out of about two thousand building employees, two had turned out to have violent criminal records, both sex crimes. In a bit of social equity Hartman enjoyed, one of the men with a criminal past was a senior executive of a securities brokerage company, while the other was a worker on the building's maintenance staff. Hartman had checked the court records for details. Neither of them had been in trouble for the past five years, but the police wouldn't give them any points for that.

He felt the rightness of the enterprise come together in his head, an arrangement of forethought and planned maneuvers that made a particular kind of music. He moved toward the office entrance, again checking the scene and Tracy's appearance and listening for the sounds of any approach.

As he walked from the office, he visualized himself slipping past the guard post, unobserved. Everything worked as he planned. Two deaths—the girl in the park and this one. Two lawsuits. Life was good.

CHAPTER SEVEN

I knocked on Jerry's door at eight in the morning. He answered right away. As I walked in, I saw Sean, paused halfway down the stairs. He glanced at me, turned, and went back up. I was no longer just one of his father's friends, a neutral adult. I was a white knight signed on to fight for the family. I had become, to this fifteen-year-old, a person of interest. I could also feel that my presence was uncomfortable for him, that I was someone he marked and feared.

Even before I was fully in the house, Jerry shoved a piece of paper into my hand. He'd gotten what we needed from Hartman.

"I had to wait hours," he said, after we took seats in the living room. "I've never sat in one place that long. There was a secretary, Bonnie something. She kept offering me coffee, asking if I wanted to leave a message, telling me Hartman might not come in. I would have left, for sure, if you hadn't told me to wait all day. He finally showed up about four o'clock."

He was excited telling me the story. The action and his accomplishments had raised his spirits.

"You were right about the file," he said. "He definitely didn't want me to see it again. He told me he'd been doing this a long time and the best thing for me was to accept the facts and let go. He'd already done everything he could to argue my case with the company, but there was no way around the decision, because Karen had . . . Hartman didn't say she lied, but—" Jerry's voice changed. "I felt like punching his lights out. I had to listen to him. He was lying. I knew that." He looked at me, still angry about it. "I wanted to kill him." He stood up. "I'm not like that." He sat down to settle himself.

"I kept at it, though, like you said. So he finally let me see the thing. But not to make a copy. He had excuses—the company had a policy about copying client files, something like that. So when he showed me the papers, I looked for what you told me to and it was all there. I remembered what I could and wrote it down." He pointed to the paper sitting on my lap. "So there it is. But I didn't get it all. There were a bunch of doctors listed, and I couldn't remember the names."

He'd remembered enough. There were two hospitals listed: Johns Hopkins, in Baltimore, and Fallston General, just outside that city. Karen had been born and raised in Baltimore. He'd written down a couple of years she'd had treatments—1981 and 1983—though not the specific dates. He also remembered Karen's health carrier—Blue Cross.

"You did a great job, Jerry," I said. "Now you can relax and stay home with the kids. Your part's over now. I know what to do next."

He didn't ask what I'd do and I didn't tell him; there was no need for that. I had brought some release-of-information forms with me. We went to a pharmacy, where Jerry signed the forms and we got them notarized. The releases would give me access to Karen's medical records at both hospitals, and also at Blue Cross.

I drove to Thirtieth Street Station and had to wait only a half hour for the train. The last time I'd been to Baltimore, it had been to see a game. I often thought about cities in terms of their ballparks. It wasn't a bad way to categorize a place. For instance, there was no doubt that New York had gone downhill since Ebbets Field had disappeared, and suffered another blow when the Polo Grounds was demolished.

I knew baseball before I knew reporting. I was a minor-league ballplayer for only three years. If I'd been able to stick with it, I might have reaped the benefits of modern-day baseball—free agency and its multimillion-dollar contracts. As a fan, I was sickened by big-money baseball; I liked to think that even if I'd made it as a player, I might not have a different point of view.

I'd had a good shot at the majors. But at twenty-one, I ripped up my shoulder and career. That alone didn't make me hate the game. Whenever I went to major-league cities I visited stadiums, an old habit I've never kicked. Baltimore used to have Memorial Field, a nice old place I liked, with real grass and trees behind the outfield wall. Memorial had been replaced by Camden Yards. It was a good-looking park, built to appear comfortably old. But behind the right-field wall, instead of grass and trees, there was an indoor mall, with fast food and fancy bars, and big-screen televisions built into the walls.

We drove past it in the cab. The Orioles were out of town, which was just as well. We went on to Johns Hopkins. The hospital's computerized patient records went back as far as 1972. I had the medical release forms and a copy of Karen's death certificate. The hospital records showed that Karen had not been treated at Johns Hopkins in 1981 or 1983, the years Jerry had seen in the file.

I checked the two years before and after. She'd been seen in the ER in 1980 for an ankle sprained in a volleyball game.

There was nothing else: no sexually transmitted diseases, no pelvic disorders, no cancer. I got another cab to Fallston General. I gave them the releases and their check came up blank. She had never been treated for anything there.

That left Baltimore Blue Cross/Blue Shield. Their records showed medical insurance for her from 1976 to 1983. In 1981 and 1983, she'd been pretty healthy. She wasn't hospitalized. She'd had checkups and routine prescriptions. They had the sprained ankle in 1980. They didn't get billed for anything else.

I caught the next Amtrak back to Philadelphia. There were credit card–operated telephones on the train. I took out my copy of Jerry's policy and called the insurance company. I worked my way up from the switchboard to an accountant in the benefits department. It took him only seconds after I gave him the policy number and the name Karen Murphy.

"We don't have that account anymore," he said. "It lapsed eight years ago."

"Eight years? I don't get it. Why did it lapse?"

"No idea why," he said. "We don't have the file anymore. You'd have to call the agent and ask."

I took a window seat and looked through my flickering reflection at the world outside. The shifting background turned my face from firm to insubstantial and back. *Ask your insurance agent.* Hartman, of course, did have the answer. I thought about con artists and their ploys. They are magicians, and their magic all sleight of hand. The basic move is always the same: They say or show that something has occurred, and make the victims prove it didn't. As all reporters know, the magicians have it easy, while the audience has it hard.

It is always easier to prove that something happened than to prove it did not. To investigate an event, you find evidence, get public records, or talk to people who were there. But there are no records of events that have never occurred. No video. No eyewitnesses. If people tell you they never saw it happen, the only thing you know is that those particular people didn't see it occur.

But with all of that going for him, Hartman had made a mistake. His lies about Karen's illness were too specific. The events in his phony file would have to have left a paper trail. If I could show the trail was missing, then I could prove that what he described had never actually taken place. Karen and Jerry's policy had ended eight years ago. That had to mean that Hartman had been keeping the premium payments since then. If I alerted the insurance company about the scam, the company wouldn't like the news but wouldn't do anything to pay Jerry what he was due. If I went to the police, Hartman might get arrested, but that wouldn't get Jerry the death benefit either. Hartman had cheated the family out of their money. I intended to see that he paid.

CHAPTER EIGHT

The sign on the door of Room 183 at City Hall, where all the wills were stored, said DEBTS AND DEDUCTIONS. It was a curious way to sum up the legacy of the dead; bureaucracy's view of the world. Probate court. I was braced for another encounter with public records, prepared to spend hours, probably days, wading through towers of paperwork, knowing I might find nothing I needed. Or something that might pay off big. But public records were always the right place to start.

People often acted as if they moved through their lives without leaving traces of where they'd been or what they'd done. Public records put the lie to all that. It was Shannon, my first editor, at the *Northampton Gazette,* who introduced me to public records, the real world's version of a crystal ball, the one that worked.

The *Gazette* was in a century-old stone building that had once been a country house. The first floor, which still looked like a large living room, was the common work space, where all the reporters and editors had their desks. When Shannon wanted to talk to a reporter alone, or isolate himself to think, he went upstairs to a small attic room. It had a wooden desk and two beat-up chairs facing a window that looked out over Main Street's two-story shops.

I had come to the paper to do sports, playing whatever angles I had left from my old life. But Shannon told me I had a reporter's eye. He thought I should do more than cover sports. He took me up to the attic one day to talk. He'd decided to give me a story no one else was interested in doing. He suggested I find out how a local branch of the state university obtained and spent its money.

"They have an annual budget of a hundred million dollars," Shannon said. "That's a lot of money. Big money always means big secrets. Let's get behind their press releases and find out what secrets they have. Start with how they get and give out grants and where the money really comes from and goes."

He always assumed hidden truths could be uncovered by anyone who had the will and skills to look.

"There are grant and contract files," he said. "Most of the money comes from federal, state, and county government. The money is public, so the records are too."

I'd never done that kind of work before. I had no idea where to start.

"It doesn't matter where you start. Just go where the records are stored, start reading, and then use common sense. If you don't know where to find something, ask someone there. People who would never give you information directly or let themselves be quoted for a story are often willing guides to their own files. Don't ever think of what you seek as a lump sum or a big prize. Look for the money in small pieces, one dollar, one contract at a time. Then look for the people who get or spend the money. You'll end up with the big picture in the end. And you'll be the only one who has it. Because no matter how open and available information is, nobody ever looks."

The job was as simple as he'd said. I read through thirty federal contracts awarded to the university's School of Education. Much of the twenty million the school had received was spent on luxury cars and conferences in fancy resorts around the world. Each expense was openly listed, along with its stated reason, and every expenditure had passed a review; there were signed acknowledgments of federal audits in the files. The way they used the money didn't seem right, but it appeared to be legal, according to the auditors. Maybe spending big money on entertainment was the way things were done in the educational world. I wasn't out of suspicions, but I was almost out of material to read. I made an interim report to Shannon. I wasn't sure where else to go.

"The answer's still in the records," he said.

So I went back to the same files and read them again, and took more notes, and when that didn't get me anywhere, I made lists. I listed the federal officials named in the files, and then all the faculty and students. I compared the names on the lists. I found that five of the federal officials were also registered as students at the university. All five had been awarded doctorates from the School of Education in the past few years, at the same time they were supervising the university contracts.

I began to understand Shannon's way. Everything in the library was a public record. Every doctoral thesis was there. I found the federal officials' completed dissertations. All five were neatly bound and looked like books but contained only the thick stack of boilerplate pages of the federal contracts that had been awarded to the university—nothing else.

It was my first big story, a huge local scandal. It had good headlines: "Doctoral degrees awarded in exchange for million-dollar federal contracts." And it hit the university hard. It didn't surprise Shannon a bit. He said there was probably nothing of value in the world that hadn't been used at one time or another as a bribe.

I spent two years working for him. Along the way, reporting became a solid replacement for the career I'd had on the ball field. But reporting was my second life that didn't last.

I was doing a human interest story about elderly people in nursing homes, impoverished and alone. I followed the money the way I knew how. I discovered a ring of doctors and lawyers using their skills to steal. They made false diagnoses of dementia, obtained guardianship of their targets, and took the money away.

It was another good story. But I never wrote it. Shannon believed I'd be a good newspaper reporter, but he was only half right. I could do all the investigating, but I didn't want to write the article. Instead, I wanted to help the victims. I used the techniques Shannon taught me and did something he couldn't understand or condone. I never wrote the story because I made a deal with the thieves instead. The old people got their money and their homes and their independence back, and in return I kept the information to myself. The thieves had even offered to pay me for my silence, but I didn't take anything. Not that time.

All Shannon really knew was that I didn't write the story. I never told him any more. He fired me, rightly so, and did everything he could to see I never worked as a reporter again. I wish I could tell him I still spend my time in the rooms with the records, where so many of the world's secrets are kept.

Room 183 was the archive for probated wills. Up front was a long, narrow counter with a faded green-felt top. There were countless file folders on the dozens of long shelves that took up the back of the room.

Eight thousand adults died in Philadelphia every year. Every death was noted by the Register of Wills, whether or not the person had a will. It was the register's office that listed and kept track of anything anyone stood to inherit. The point of all that record keeping was to collect the state's share, the inheritance tax. I'd never worked this particular room before. It was a while before a thin young guy came to the counter and asked if he could help.

"How many cases can I request at a time?" I asked.

The clerk smiled. "Sky's the limit." Working alone in the quiet must suit him, I thought. "Makes no difference to me," he added. "You have any particular names in mind?"

Hartman was the only name I had, but nothing here would be filed under his name.

"How about the most recently filed cases? Do you keep them chronologically?"

"Not exactly," he answered. "But if you look in the index card file in the cabinet behind you"—he pointed to it—"you'll find cases filed by date. You write down the names you want, and then I pull them for you."

I turned to the cabinet. I picked ten cases, still following Shannon's rules: It doesn't matter where you begin. It took me four hours to read through them all. When the stack was done, I had the feel of the files. Six of them were thin: a routine, simple listing of the dead person's assets and a copy of the will.

But four of the files were thicker, because it wasn't clear exactly what property the dead person owned, or exactly how much everything was worth. In those cases, a probate official had been appointed to find answers to those questions. The official gathered the information by holding interviews with relatives and others and examining bank records. The paperwork documenting the newly gathered information was then added to the file.

The thickest files were cases in which survivors asked the register's office to change the way the funds and property were to be distributed. In other words, they were challenging the will. The procedure was much like a trial; the probate official decided between the competing claims. Usually, the richer the estate, the greater the number of claims made. And the more disputes, the larger the file. When a half-dozen or more family members argued over the leavings, all kinds of family stories ended up in the file, available to the interested public forevermore.

I read a bunch of the thick files. One contained copies of passionate letters to three different lovers. Another will had memos attached in which the departed described friends and business partners in unflattering terms. For some people, dying was yet another opportunity for anger. There were depositions from sons and daughters claiming their parents were liars, or crooks, or molesters. Mash notes from and about the dead.

I took a break for lunch, then got back to the records. Familiarity made me faster at going through them. There was still no mention of Hartman, but I found a case similar to Jerry's at first glance.

A probate official had found an insurance policy listed in the dead man's assets, but no death benefit had been paid. The official had to determine why there was no death benefit. An insurance company representative was quoted as saying the man's medical history had been concealed. He had taken out the policy only four months before he died and had failed to mention in his application that he had pancreatic cancer. It wasn't an insurance company scam but a dying man desperate to leave something behind.

I left at five. I'd found nothing on Hartman yet. I was back the next morning at nine. I spent the next three days the same way, and got through two hundred files.

On midmorning of the third day I finally came across Hartman's name. James Johnson of the Bustleton section of Northeast Philadelphia had died. He was a sixty-six-year-old grandfather of seven and father of three. The largest asset listed in the probate records was a three-hundred-thousand-dollar life insurance policy payable to the estate. The death benefit was not paid. The probate official took statements in his office, and this time the insurance company representative was Jim Hartman. He said the family voided the insurance by missing a string of monthly premium payments.

By the fourth day, I had come across Hartman's name three more times. In each case, a family had not received death benefits on policies Hartman sold. In one case, there were too many missed payments again; in another, false information had been given in applying; in the third, too much money had been taken out in loans. I'd never realized insurance policies could get canceled in so many different ways.

Now I had the names of some of Hartman's clients. Their families couldn't be too happy about what had occurred. I wondered if any of them had tried to do something about the benefit they'd never been paid. Probate court wasn't a place that helped people put things right. It was called a court, and it had officials who acted like judges, but justice wasn't the point. All that mattered there was pinning down assets and collecting taxes due. To wage a fight, the families would have to have brought their complaint to a lawyer and then to civil court.

It was easy to look up. The civil court record room was in the same building, one flight up. In this case, the room, big as it was, contained only a very small part of the actual files. There was a card catalog up front, and also a computer terminal, which accessed the names and docket numbers of every civil case. But files that went back more than a few years were stored in a huge warehouse space on the ninth floor. I'd been in that particular record room many times.

I ran the four names I had through the computer. I felt well satisfied when one of them showed up. It was "Stein, J. PC 91063." It wasn't until I pulled the file that I realized the first initial was different from the name of the man who had been insured by Hartman. Yet the home address was the same. The probate case was about the will of Robert Stein, who had died of a heart attack two years ago. The civil case was about John Stein, twenty-four years old. He had died in a bicycle accident six months after his father. I flipped through the file.

John Stein had been riding his bike one night and had hit a bump in the road at the intersection of Frankford and Torresdale Avenues. The front wheel of his bike got stuck in an old trolley track, and he was thrown from the bike and then run over by a city bus.

The family hired a lawyer and filed a suit. I took down the lawyer's name, Rachel Curren. She had already started working; the file had in it the allegations that begin a lawsuit, and the city's response. There was also a police report of the accident, an autopsy report, and some photographs of the street scene on the day the man died.

The suit claimed the road was in disrepair, that the unused trolley track should have been paved over long ago, and that there was a similar accident at the same intersection three years before and the city hadn't done anything to repair the street. According to the suit, the city's negligence therefore caused the death, and the city ought to pay. The case was moving through the court system slowly, as most civil cases do. The trial was not yet scheduled.

There were thousands of similar suits against the city every year, although most of them didn't involve a death. Every time someone got injured on city property, the city got sued. The cases were so common, lawyers had a name for the category: slip and fall. I knew about them—all reporters did—because the victims were always trying to get us to write about their accidents. We rarely did.

I had a feeling about the case. I didn't resist it. I glanced around. There were a few people in the room, none close to me. I took the reports and the photos and tucked them under my shirt. No one would notice or care that the materials were gone. It was just one file, one death.

CHAPTER NINE

I followed my feeling about the Stein case all the way to Mt. Airy. I had called the lawyer, Rachel Curren, and that's where her office was. It wasn't a business area. Mt. Airy was a residential section of the city, a neighborhood of stone and brick houses with large lawns that looked less urban and less poor than it actually was.

The address was on a side street about a block and a half off Lincoln Drive, the neighborhood's busiest road. It wasn't a grand location, but it didn't matter where a lawyer's office was or what it looked like. People didn't choose their lawyers that way. People picked lawyers because a friend recommended someone who had gotten results. Outcome was all that mattered. Their personalities also didn't mean much, because people didn't like lawyers anyway. Lawyers were hired assassins; they weren't supposed to be likable, simply willing and able to kill.

Rachel Curren's house was a small, single-family home of stone and wood. A brick path led to the side entrance, where there was a white LAW OFFICE sign. I knocked on the glass door but there was no response, so after a minute I pulled it open and looked in.

A strikingly beautiful blonde was sitting at a desk across the room, telephone receiver tucked between shoulder and ear. It was hard not to stare. She was pretty enough to be a model but more filled out and stronger. Weight lifter Barbie, I thought. She looked my way and waved me in. The wave was accompanied by a smile. I wasn't sure if she was the woman I had come to see, but I was motivated to find out.

The office was a single large room. The part of it she was in had an oriental rug, a nice maple desk, and two matching chairs. All of the furniture was on the rug, as if it had come in one piece. There wasn't anywhere else to sit, so I moved up close and settled into one of the chairs.

She stayed on the phone for a minute. I didn't have to overhear much to know she was the lawyer. In that brief interval, I heard her say reassuringly that the call wasn't on the clock, and suggest that maybe a problem could be resolved by the client's simply talking to the other side. That meant she was violating two principal rules of lawyering, as I understood it: to build up billable hours and always to file a lawsuit.

When the call ended, I introduced myself. I hadn't said much about what my business was, but it didn't seem to bother her.

"Rachel Curren." She held out her hand. She didn't leave it with me long, but it left a firm impression. Her hair was long but tied back. Her legs were popping muscles, suggesting a runner or biker. She was dressed simply—white shirt, blue skirt. Simple looked good.

"I was listening to the end of your call," I said, and I told her what I thought.

She laughed. "I didn't think a lawsuit was going to solve that one, Mr. Gray. And I didn't think billing was going to get me much."

"You mean you were talking to a poor person with a weak case? That's unusual, too."

This time she only grinned. "I take it you did notice we're not in Center City. Clients around here tend not to be rich. That usually makes their cases weaker."

"So what's a poor lawyer to do?"

She took that one seriously. She picked up a file off her desk. I knew she wasn't going to hand it to me or show it to me. Holding it signaled that what was inside meant something to her.

"This guy," she said. "Typical of what I get. Fifty years old. Alone, in every way that matters. Handicapped. Has a job, though. And he has a place to live. Good enough to get by in the world. Until a little landlord-tenant dispute."

"Let me guess," I said. "No money and a weak case."

She nodded. "Caught in the wheels."

She said it low, as if to herself. I asked anyway.

"The wheels?"

"Just a way I think about it," she said. "The city's in better shape lately, and that raises demand for housing, and that means landlords can charge more, and the end result of the whole wonderful process is that Joe here"—she motioned at the file—"gets asked to pay a little more for the privilege of living in a Philadelphia slum."

Anger had a bad reputation these days, but not with me. There's anger that's like love. That's the kind that when someone gets hurt, someone else says, "I'm not going to stand for another minute of it." It was the anger of angels. A lot of good work gets done when people get mad. She was angry that way.

"The wheel turns," I said. "So you stop the wheel."

She nodded again. "Without a lawyer, he's another homeless man. With one, maybe not."

"I get the feeling you'll find a little something to do for him."

She tapped the folder with her finger, as if the case needed to get solved right away, and she didn't have the patience. Then the grin came back. "Maybe I'll offer the landlady a subsidy to let him stay," she said, "or give him some help to find another place in the area."

"And pay for it yourself?"

"Maybe that's what the fees from the better-paying clients are for."

I couldn't tell whether she was kidding. I didn't think she was.

"So that's what I do," she said. "What about you? You said on the phone you were looking into one of my cases. You're not a cop or you would have said so. You're a private investigator, then?"

I usually say I'm a reporter, freely using credentials I no longer have. I'm used to that particular lie. Instead, I told her some of the truth. I had done that more than once lately. It wasn't a habit that would serve me well.

"No. I just look into things for friends. Sometimes I even do it for strangers."

"What do you do when you finish looking?"

"I get people their money back, if that's what they've lost," I said.

"And do you get paid for helping your friends in this way?"

"When I get back the money, I make sure there's a little extra there and keep that for myself."

"So you're not just a nice guy," she said.

"I am a nice guy. But I need money. I'm always fixing my house."

"You don't run into too many nice people these days," she said.

"That's true, but that's because we probably spend too much time with the wrong crowd. I know I do."

I realized I didn't want to bring up John Stein. It was going to break the spell. But I didn't have a choice about that.

"You mentioned John Stein on the phone," she said. "Was he one of your friends?"

I decided to stop telling truths.

"Yes," I said. "I knew him."

"So you came to check me out?"

"The family's been through a lot. His father died, you know, just six months before John did."

"I agree with you," she said. "Two deaths, a lot of misfortune in a short time. But it's a strong case. We clearly have the city's negligence for causing the accident with the bike. Mrs. Stein is the only one left in the family, which might limit a bit what we're able to get. But she's not that old, she was terribly harmed, and we ought to be able to get her a lot."

I tried again. "I just want to believe she's finally going to get a break, after everything that's happened. Did you know that after the father died, the family never received the death benefit from their insurance company?"

"No," she said. "I didn't know that. It's a shame. I hope it gets resolved."

"I'm working on it," I said.

I was giving her every chance to mention more about the insurance angle or give me a sign she was covering up. But she kept doing neither, in the most straightforward way.

"The John Stein case is very strong," she said again. "And I've had success with similar cases. I'm fairly sure there'll be a large settlement or verdict for Mrs. Stein."

"I guess this'll be one of those cases that lets you help the poor ones out."

She agreed. "That would be good."

I wondered how much farther to go. I didn't want to mention Hartman or ask about fraud. I wasn't ready for Hartman yet. And if she was part of it, despite the feeling I had about her, I wasn't ready for her.

The phone rang. As she took the call, I got up and walked away from the desk, succeeding in not listening to this one. Once was enough.

I looked around the room to see signs of how she lived. In the far corner of the room were stairs leading up to the rest of the house. I assumed she lived here with her family. But a second later, I realized my guess had been wrong. People have houses for lots of reasons. It sometimes has to do with feeling a little more stable in the world. I was single and had a house. In addition, in my case, I liked to be able to rebuild the places I lived in, and they didn't like it much when you did that with rentals.

I glanced over. She was involved in the call. She cupped the phone.

"I've got to take this call," she said. "But is there anything else?"

"Not right now. But can I call you again?"

I had asked her that without knowing whether I only meant business.

"Yes," she said. She hadn't asked me why.

I exited up the stone steps and out toward Lincoln Drive. I

felt distracted and on edge, and I knew exactly why. It had nothing to do with insurance fraud or lawyers. I was thrown more than a little by having a totally unexpected encounter with somebody I felt attracted to. Another chance encounter with a saint.

I walked down the street, a ghost at my side. I was remembering a remarkable day I'd spent with Karen. Time hadn't erased it.

It was a sunny afternoon in late fall, warmer than usual that year. We decided to walk past the waterfall and up one of the wooded hills. We made our own path through the trees and bushes and found a small clearing.

I took off my coat and we used it for a blanket. The thick foliage seemed to still the air, quiet all sounds.

I didn't have to reach for her. She came to me instead, her body tight against mine. We kissed. Her hands were on my face, over my ears. I remember the warmth and silence.

She undressed quickly, keeping herself close, removing the barrier between us, a thin wall she tore down. When she was naked, she moved back to let me see. She was pretty and strong, wiry muscles, soft belly, small breasts. I undressed, more slowly, but as urgently as she.

When the sex was over, we didn't move apart. There wasn't the usual rush to cover up, the sense that sharing had been a little too much, the cues to move to a safer distance, the compelling impulse to put on clothes.

We shared secrets instead. She showed me a long, deep scar on her thigh. She'd gotten it when she was eleven, in summer camp. She convinced another girl to sneak out with her for an unsupervised early-morning river swim. She'd cut herself on an underwater rock, jumping in to keep the girl from drowning. She liked the scar, and the lesson. She'd gotten a friend in trouble; she'd done what she needed to get her out. In turn, I told her what I really did.

The late-afternoon rush-hour street sounds of Lincoln Drive jolted me out of my reverie. I was oblivious to the steps I'd taken for blocks. I was forgetting the present, immersed again in the past.

CHAPTER TEN

It was a Wednesday morning when Jim Hartman got a call from Rachel Curren. She felt obligated to let him know that an investigator had visited her about the Steins. He wondered how much her visitor knew and if a great money run might be coming to an end. If so, he would deal with the situation soon enough. He cradled the phone and went back to his computer. He enjoyed this part of his work too much to delay it.

Wednesday was his major workday at the office, the day he spent boosting his accounts. It was not always necessary to take physical risks to complete his scams. He could steal electronically as easily as he could in person.

He always did an hour of completely legitimate on-line trading first, allowing a small portion of that time for speculating with stocks. Taking one outright risk every Wednesday morning for the past several years had paid off well. He was good at synthesizing what he read in *The New York Times* and *The Wall Street Journal* and matching those insights to the fate of businesses.

This morning he had bought five thousand shares of Cine-Od on the New York Exchange. The company owned a national chain of movie theaters. He was betting that Sony or one of the other entertainment megacorporations would soon gobble it up. If so, his investment could pay off big. He wished he could influence the process more directly but he didn't have that level of power, at least not yet.

By eleven in the morning, he had left the arena of uncontrollable risk. He moved on to making easy money, a strategy as good as printing dollars or writing cashable checks to himself. Life insurance was perfect for his purposes. He called up his files of policies, all legitimately sold. As the names scrolled by he could picture each family, and recall the work he had done to build up a customer base. All good theft began with sales. But if selling was all you did, you started and stayed a fool. His father had followed that route in life, one Hartman had discarded after observing it up close.

His Lotus Notes calendar identified policies that had reached five years' maturity within the past month. There were twelve. These policies were legitimate. For the past five years, these clients had paid on average three to four hundred dollars a month for a much as half a million dollars in whole-life insurance. The deal-making hook in selling whole-life policies was the equity or savings you were supposed to accumulate. But as with so much in the insurance business, the customer's expectation arose from unclear words.

The actual contract was written in a way that was infinitely subject to change. When the insurance company changed the terms, the customer had no way to know what had been done. And all the money the clients put in—twenty or thirty thousand dollars each so far, as well as the interest earned—wouldn't be available to them for another five years.

He called up the cover page on the first client. The Bauers were a couple he had first met at Sportsters, a local restaurant and bar. Most of his contacts with customers were social at the start. That was the best way to sell.

He split the screen so he could work on two files at once. On the left was the Bauers' original policy. On the right was a new policy form. He pressed a preset shortcut key and watched as the software took all of the Bauers' information from the left-hand side of the screen and copied it onto the blank form. In effect, he was writing a new policy for them, without their knowledge or consent. By doing so, he instantly made forty-two hundred dollars, an agent's commission for the first year's sale of a policy the Bauers' size. The family still had the same exact coverage; that hadn't changed. But their savings had decreased by the forty-two hundred that went to Hartman.

It only took him twenty minutes to do the same thing twelve times over and put fifty thousand dollars in his own accounts. The practice was called churning, because it made money by constantly turning things over, the way farmers made butter. It wasn't legal, but it was a common industry practice. And no insurance agent had ever been arrested for this kind of theft. On the rare occasion a clever customer caught on to the trick, the only thing the agents and companies ever had to do was pay the money back. There couldn't be an easier or safer way to steal. And he'd been stealing every way he could since he was a child.

By the time his parents died, Hartman had gotten from them everything they were capable of giving. Their love was voluntary; he had taken the rest. They raised him, but they didn't know him. He developed and learned at the edges of their awareness, preyed on aspects of their daily lives to which they paid insufficient attention. With their checkbooks and account numbers and the knowledge that neither parent kept close track of their available funds, he started withdrawing a hundred dollars a month from their joint account. He was twelve.

Before that, he had already begun to do business of his own. He sold his father's cigarettes and liquor to neighborhood kids. He could have moved on to other drugs but chose not to because it wasn't a business he could control. There were too many dangers.

He kept all of the money in a metal box in a hole in the ground under a sagging part of the wooden porch so low in the middle that only someone as thin as he could reach it. He critiqued these early efforts now with the amused wisdom of an older perspective. He should have split the money into two piles in case one was discovered. He should have made sure his parents' account numbers were written down and left in a plausible suspect's house. By the time he was fifteen, he no longer made such mistakes.

His father was an auto parts distributor who never made much money. The boy dismissed him for his weakness. His mother annoyed him less; she neither achieved nor failed. But there was nothing there to admire or learn. She depended on his father for money; in return she listened to his rambling complaints. Hartman knew about sex and what it meant, but it wasn't necessary to marry for that. It was never clear to him what either of them wanted, of each other or of him.

His father died when Hartman was twenty, his mother eleven years later. Before their deaths, they had signed on loans that milked every drop of equity out of the house. He'd used the funds to open his office and to lease his first car, a Cadillac.

His first adult business decision turned out to be his best, the one that had sustained him through the years. It allowed him to focus his efforts, to cast a smaller shadow and steal as much as he wanted, to lessen his exposure by acquiring a cover. It was hard to imagine one better. He bought himself the right to put a sign on the glass window of his first small office in the northeast section of Philadelphia: He was an agent for Bethlehem Casualty & Life.

He knew he needed protection, that there were going to be confrontations. To make money, he intended to create victims, as many as he could. There was always the possibility of a bitter, violent response. He was smart but not especially big. Money could buy protection. If he could acquire enough money, he could have the police, or even an army, defend him. But it would take years to get that big.

He solved his problem by learning to fight. He picked a karate school he could get to every day. He was a good student from the start, smart enough to focus on what he needed to learn and disciplined enough to devote himself to the learning. Motivation wasn't a problem. He found it appealing that hurting people had a technique. He was usually among the best in the classes he took, and for over twenty years he'd never stopped.

And although his focus was always on the money and his plans to make it, there was more to his life. There were people who considered him a colleague, who thought of themselves as his friends, and there were women. He enjoyed the company, the work and the sex. But people were more important to him than that. He made it a point to use everyone he ever knew. They either had money or power, or were a means to get something important he wanted. And the best, most useful person he had ever met was the lawyer Rachel Curren.

He had met her through a judge, a man with whom Hartman did business. She was beautiful, but seemed oblivious to her own appearance. If she had appreciated herself, she wouldn't have been after transformation. She spent obsessive amounts of time working out. It wasn't hard for him to make a connection. To his surprise, there was a coldness in her that matched his own. They went out a few times. She didn't reveal much directly but he didn't need her to. Between the judge, their conversations, and a casual inspection of her apartment, he was able to develop the rest.

He felt inspired. She was a perfect resource, capable and flawed, the qualities so separate. He sometimes watched her in the courtroom. She managed information and people with the clarity and focus of a machine. She worked without emotion. He was good at seeing those kinds of truths. Clients and juries didn't seem to notice. They attributed caring to her gender, and strength to her looks. At night, she shifted from restraint to an appetite for stimulation. She spent hours on a circuit that included hot new clubs in the northern Liberties section of the city. She had two completely different states of mind, and alcohol to help her shift between the two.

He enjoyed her company, but most of all he enjoyed the effect of her company on others. He was amused to see that his sales went up when he made contacts in her presence. Even better was the sense of having a great mystery to solve, how to get the most out of the resource on which he had stumbled. He didn't have a use for her at first but was eager to find one. She was a key he could use to unlock one of society's doors and let money tumble through. And then he thought of the ideal scheme.

His solution was murders made to look like accidents. He soon found he enjoyed the murders more than the thefts. But he knew he had to stay focused on the money. Because money meant business, and business—unlike passion—always required clear thinking. He needed clear thinking to stay safe. Rachel's settlements and verdicts had netted him the biggest paydays of his career, three million dollars in the past five years. Of course, her share of the bounty was even greater, an undesirable but unavoidable outcome from Hartman's point of view. Eventually he would come up with some way of relieving her of those funds as well, though he hadn't worked out his plan as yet.

Meanwhile, she had been the ideal partner, the alchemist's stone that turned the victims he created into riches. But she could also, if needed, become an ideal suspect for all the staged deaths. If things went wrong, as anything could, she could block any suspicion that came his way. The visitor she'd just had might mean that day had come. If necessary, she alone would take the fall.

CHAPTER ELEVEN

The building that housed Bethlehem Casualty & Life was huge, gleaming marble and granite. The bottom floors of the sixty-eight-story building were filled with retail businesses: bank branches, clothing boutiques, an exotic flower shop, and an assortment of other upscale stores.

Only a few years earlier all that stood on this particular ground was a ramshackle building, a once fine Victorian structure that died of vandalism and neglect. A group of speculators let the building rot until someone wanted the land under it badly enough to pay the speculators' price. In the meantime the public put up with a deteriorating, dangerous eyesore. Making the public pay the price for private real estate speculation was a time-honored way to get rich in Philadelphia.

I was there to test some suspicions. If John Stein had pursued his father's missing death benefit, he might have made himself into a target by threatening to uncover Hartman's scam. I had strong suspicions but no real evidence.

The two obvious places to go next were Hartman's insurance branch office and the main office of the insurance company. It was reasonably likely the insurance company wasn't in the business of committing murders or even dealing in the phony insurance policies issued to Stein's father, Jerry, and the others on Hartman's list. But I needed information to pin things down and the company was the place to start.

The office was up in the clouds, beginning on the fortieth floor. Two gleaming teak doors inscribed in brass announced the company name and all of the countries in which it did business. In a reception area beyond, two women were seated at a low desk. They seemed less like workers than observers of the passing social scene, curious about anyone who might pop out of the elevator on their floor.

I gave my name to the one on the left and asked to see someone to discuss the life insurance policy of the deceased Robert Stein. She asked who I was, and in particular whether I was an agent.

"I'm a reporter doing an article for *The Philadelphia Inquirer*," I said.

No matter who said it, there was no way to call that particular line a lie. Anyone could call himself or herself a reporter—it wasn't a licensed term. And anyone could be doing an article for the *Inquirer* or any other newspaper in the world. Many articles in newspapers were written by freelance writers. They had no credentials, and their claims were invulnerable to verification. Calling a newspaper to check was useless; between the freelancers, the part-timers, and the normal staff, there was no way to tell.

"Okay," she immediately said. "I'll have someone come out and see you."

She dialed a number while I stood there. I knew where the phone was ringing. She was calling public relations, that part of every big company whose sole mission was to make the company look good. For that reason, PR usually knew less about what really happened at a company than anyone else.

I had barely begun to settle in when a friendly woman in a

dark gray suit introduced herself as Renee from public relations. She smiled a lot and led me off to her domain.

Her area was quiet and very nice. PR offices always were, whatever the looks and reality of the rest of the place. She sat down and I did too.

"So," she said, "what's this about?"

She was still friendly and I knew she would stay that way, no matter what I said. I made up what I told her, but it was steeped in the life I'd lived, so it had the ring of truth.

"Well, Renee, this didn't start out to be about insurance or your company," I said. "It's one of those stories we're doing to increase circulation, you know, making the local editions more community friendly. The story is about a day in the life of one city block. We interview all the families on a particular street, take a human interest approach. People like to read about themselves and their neighbors. It sells papers."

She nodded a lot as I spoke. I was essentially explaining what she did for a living. She seemed to like that.

"I'm doing Sedgeley Street in Frankford, where we have a new section coming out. Everything was fine until we got to one of the families, the Steins. Turns out this particular family had a tragedy to tell. Our promotional angle started turning into a real story. The father and his grown son both died in the past two years. The old man had a heart attack. The kid, twenty-four, died in a bike accident six months after that. The family had a policy with your company for the old man. One of our editors got interested in that."

Her smile finally faded a bit. PR always tried to help a reporter do a story when the company name might appear in print. They were looking for the best spin possible. But if a story was trouble for the company, she couldn't do more than spin. That's when she'd turn me over to someone else. That's where I wanted to get. She asked me to go on, still hoping for a friendly angle. I gave her the rest.

"Apparently, there was something wrong with the policy, because the family never collected any death benefit."

I could see her shift to a more anxious mode. There could be an article in the city's biggest newspaper suggesting that the company did something wrong. That was a PR office's worst case. I knew she was going to leave the room to seek advice. She stood up.

"Let me see if I can get you some specific information," she said, more professional than friendly. "I'll be right back."

It took ten minutes. I knew what was happening. All reporters knew how these things worked. She was talking to community relations or somebody else above PR. That person would try to find out what the company knew about my situation. And it wouldn't be to help my story but to see whether there was any damage to be controlled. They'd find the place in the company where any information on the Steins was stored and quickly find out the very things I needed to know. They wouldn't want to tell me much of what they found. But they'd give me a piece of it, probably enough to try to throw me off track.

Renee returned, took me to the elevators and into one going up. She held a credit card–sized electronic key and inserted it into a slot between the first forty lit numbers and the remaining twenty-eight. She didn't press any of the buttons; there must have been a language the car and the card both spoke.

We stopped at forty-eight. She took me into a large, elegant waiting room, a big step up from the one downstairs. She said Mr. Hundley would be with me shortly. She asked me to wait.

Her voice got so lost in the size of the place, I took it for a whisper.

Being asked to wait is the second most frequent request I get; number one, by far, is being asked to leave. There were three other people in the waiting area, so far away we would have needed bus passes to have a conversation. I looked out the floor-to-ceiling windows at one of the better Philadelphia views.

Straight down was Logan Circle, a quarter of an acre of flowers in bloom, a Greek god statue, a fountain shooting sprays of water high in the air. In the distance, for miles, were too many blocks of north Philadelphia, its unemployment, missing services, and battered survivors as invisible from up here as they were evident down there. From far enough away, the city was a thing of spare beauty—neat rows of houses, pristine roads, orderly trails of cars, an occasional patch of empty land.

While I waited, I braced myself for an encounter with a smooth company lawyer. That's who the spokesmen invariably were at this level of luxury and concern. And this tower was the right setting for the meeting. It was the kind of place where the myths about lawyers seemed true. The reality about lawyers, I happened to know, was very much different and worse.

There were a lot of lawyers in the world; sixteen thousand in Philadelphia alone. A good proportion of them labored in more humble surroundings, struggling to make a routine living. In fact, there were a thousand Philadelphia lawyers who did better collecting unemployment than they did working at the profession they didn't love. The truth about ambulance chasing was right there: It wasn't something lawyers did for the thrill of the hunt or because they were competitive, greedy types. To survive, they had to hunt down legal work.

The threat of poverty was also the reason many lawyers did whatever it took to get on the good side of judges. For some lawyers, getting appointed by a judge to defend a homicide case and getting the state's small payment for the job—four thousand dollars—was the financial high point of the year. And even getting the assignment was a lot of work. Favors for politicians and judges were required to keep a reasonable flow of appointed cases coming their way. They had to contribute to judges' campaigns with money they'd otherwise use for luxuries such as housing and food. They spent hours attending political functions and doing scut work for ward leaders, committeemen, and court officials. And the big payoff for all that groveling was the chance to spend three tense months or so hanging out with a murderer or rapist.

Only a select group, the brightest, the hardiest, the ones with the best connections, ended up making it to the kind of place in which I stood. Once those lawyers got their place in the tower, they held on very, very tight. For a big lawyer, job security was even more important than money, at least at first. They all knew what it was like to be a lawyer in the real world, and they never, ever wanted to go back.

I looked out the windows again, at the jewel all cities became at this height and distance. In a short while, a young woman walked in and offered to take me to see Mr. Hundley. I followed her.

The halls we walked were lined with sculptures and paintings, and occasional office-sized glass cubes in which sat well-dressed secretaries. They looked up as we walked by, in case we might need something we didn't already have. Almost all of the offices we passed had their doors open. They each had floor-to-ceiling windows. We finally stopped at one of the entryways, and before I could do anything about it, my escort was gone. I was standing at the threshold of one of the larger offices. A man got up from a desk and came toward the door to greet me.

"Richard Hundley," he said, holding out his hand.

The greetings were short and polite and then he got me settled into a seat by his desk. We both had the window view but he kept his attention on me. He was a middle-aged white man, as almost all corporate lawyers are. He looked trim, which might have been required of insurance company executives.

I didn't have to say much. He already knew exactly why I was there and what he planned to tell me. But that was fine with me. I wasn't there to argue but to learn.

"I understand you're working on a story for the *Inquirer* and we'd like to do everything we can to help," he said. "But I'm certain you understand that this is private business and all of our records are confidential. Under the circumstances, I think I can give you some valuable information, but I have to have a promise from you."

I knew what it was, but I asked anyway.

"What is it?"

"Everything I tell you must be off the record," he said.

It was an extremely frequent condition for people who wanted to talk to reporters. What it meant, if I agreed, was that nothing the person said could be quoted or used in the story. It was a contract I no longer had a right to enter into, but he didn't know that. When I was a reporter, I rarely agreed to go off the record. My goal in those days was to get information I could publish in the paper. I wasn't only after what was true, but what was documented and on the record. I had learned, from Shannon and from experience, that if I took enough time and did enough work, I could convince people to give me their information on the record. Or I could get the information from public records or other people in ways I could openly use.

Unfortunately, most reporters agreed to go off the record most of the time. A lot of reporters believed that if they had off-the-record information, they could write a story that implied the truth, using the small amount of on-the-record material they already possessed. The problem with that approach was that it usually led to a weak story or no story. Worse, going off the record created a relationship between reporters and sources based on secrecy. It was an intoxicating invitation to a private relationship with the kind of people who would never want anything important officially revealed.

Hundley was waiting for an answer.

"Sure, off the record," I said.

The lawyer nodded. He already had a file open on his desk. He moved some papers around and looked at me. "We do have a file on the Stein policy," he said. "I've already read through all of it, so let me summarize it for you. I can't actually give you this document, but everything I'm telling you comes right out of it."

I nodded in approval.

"Eighteen months ago," he continued, "six months after Mr. Stein died, the man's son came up to our office. He met with several of our people and was upset and hostile. He was certain his family had been defrauded. We explained that the problem was his father's policy had lapsed after only one year, for non-payment of premiums, years before he died. There was absolutely nothing we could do.

"When he continued insisting we should pay the death benefit, we called the agent who sold the policy to the Steins—Jim

Hartman in Northeast Philadelphia. He's been one of our agents for years, sold hundreds of policies, and never had a problem."

He stopped checking the file. "Here's the part I really want you to be careful with. You'll see why this is so confidential." He waited for me to indicate agreement. A nod seemed to do it. He went on.

"The agent has known the family for a long time. According to him, they're very dysfunctional, irrational people, very temperamental. He told us the young man had been to his office as well, extremely angry, and harassed several employees there.

"Obviously, we don't know the family situation, or what his own family told him about his father's death, the policy, and the money. But he clearly came to us with a lot of misinformation. In his mind, some terrible injustice or injury had occurred, and we became the cause. These aren't things we want to say publicly about a family that's suffered enough. But we weren't to blame."

I could sense his satisfaction. He'd not only painted his company in the best possible light, he'd also provided me with good reason not to pursue the story. His part of the job was done. I said I understood, and then I left.

On the way out, I thought it through. The company never had a problem with Hartman's story about the Steins. Its priority was business as usual, not uncovering corruption. It was the perfect partner for someone with a scam. The victims were Hartman's, not theirs, though they provided his means, his prey, and good cover. If John Stein was trouble for the scheme, his subsequent death by accident conveniently solved Hartman's problem. That meant it might not have been an accident at all.

CHAPTER TWELVE

A lot of the anguish a city reporter is drawn into starts with the ringing of a doorbell at the front of a row house. In this case, the row house was two stories and red brick. Often, whatever the time or reason for the visit, it is a middle-aged woman who answers the door. In these households, they mostly understand why you are there and welcome you in. They are always victims. They are usually people I discover I like.

The effect of their hospitality on a reporter is to make you feel vulnerable. What happened to them could happen to me, the voice inside me always said. The reporter's impulse is to apologize for being present, to atone verbally for being in a business that requires you to intrude on people's lives. The excuse—and I had used it to comfort myself, as all reporters did—is that you will tell a story that needs to be told. Without you, you come to believe, there are no lessons learned from misfortune.

"Yes?" John Stein's mother had dark hair, a round face, and a serious expression. She was in her late forties or early fifties, short, wearing loose-fitting pants in a flowery print and a T-shirt so large she disappeared inside. She opened the door wide. Her losses hadn't made her cautious. I reminded myself my intentions were good, but I introduced myself as a reporter. I said I was writing about the poor condition of the city's dangerous intersections, and that I was interested in her son's tragic accident.

"Please," she said, "come in."

She led the way back to the living room. "Let me get you some coffee. It will only be a minute."

Bethlehem Casualty & Life had a few billion more in assets and they hadn't offered me a thing. I sat in a comfortable, cushioned chair in the small living room and thought about the questions I would have had to ask if I actually were a reporter. "Mrs. Stein," I would say, "when you didn't get the insurance payment and you had no other money coming in, were you afraid you were going to lose the house? What did that feel like?" I would have been after a colorful story for readers. But I wasn't willing to sit with people that way anymore. I was no longer interested in telling the story; I wanted to fix the hurt.

She came out with a platter: Danish, cookies, a white pot and two cups. She sat on the couch and we both ate. I talked about unrepaired streets, about potholes, trolley tracks, and other dangers. I said these were problems that needed attention. She agreed. Then I moved on.

"When your husband died and you couldn't collect on his insurance, I guess you learned about that from your agent, Jim Hartman. I was wondering how well you know him."

If she asked me why I'd gone in this direction, I wasn't sure if I'd make something up.

"We've had insurance with him a long time. Fifteen years," she said.

"Did you have insurance for your son as well?"

"No," she said. "Not for Johnny."

I flinched when she softened him that way.

"Did Mr. Hartman know your son?"

"Oh, yes. Johnny was around sometimes when Mr. Hartman came by. When my husband died and we didn't get the money, Johnny was very upset. I tried to understand. There were mistakes. He—Mr. Hartman—explained. My husband hadn't kept up the payments. I could see how that could happen. It was harder for my son.

"They had arguments. Johnny thought we were being cheated. He tried to tell me, but I never understood how." She looked at me, wistful about something. "I never realized life insurance could be so uncertain." She said it low. She wasn't talking to me, I thought, but apologizing to her son for whatever sins of disbelief she thought she had committed. As a parent, it was easy to fill up with regret.

"It usually isn't uncertain," I said. "That's one reason we're looking at your case, to find out why you didn't get the life insurance money. This would be a separate story entirely. There are other families in the city whose death benefits were also denied. We may even be able to find a way to get you the insurance money you're due."

She looked puzzled.

"Sometimes when we do investigations for our stories, it results in compensation. It's not common, but it happens."

"That would be wonderful," she said.

She hadn't asked for a thing. Innocence ought to be rewarded. She'd been hit hard twice. Her son had accused Hartman of cheating them out of their money, so Hartman had certainly benefited from his death. Thieves and bullies were on a constant cruise for marks. And they never stopped taking until the well was dry.

I recalled with anger the insurance company executive's satisfied formulation that the Stein family was psychologically flawed. It was so convenient and so typical to think that John Stein's anger was built on an obsession with some imaginary injustice. It was the easy explanation. Harder to accept was the notion that an entire family had been ravaged by predators. I didn't find it difficult to take sides.

I found a right time to leave and drove to the scene of John Stein's death. I took I-95 up to Bridge Street, where the landscape was old, empty factories and warehouses, most of them boarded up. In a mile or so, the terrain became gentler: small, simple houses with neat, square front yards. I turned left on Frankford and saw two thin, white-haired old men working a small community garden set right on the grounds of a cemetery. In Philadelphia, people grew things anywhere they could. A mile beyond that was where Stein had died.

The accident site was a Philadelphia specialty: the jumbo intersection. A kid setting up a toy train collision couldn't have laid the tracks any better. There were four different streets— three of them heavily traveled—meeting at one point. Frankford was one of the city's major bus routes. Torresdale was always flooded with trucks. Hunting Park Avenue funneled kids from Northeast Catholic High School a block away. The constant heavy traffic rubbed the pavement raw and turned up stones; it needed a lot more upkeep than it got. If the case got to court, Rachel Curren could prove negligence simply by showing jurors a city road map with its wild, crossing lines.

I had the papers I'd stolen from the civil court file. The police report said that John Stein hit a rough patch, flew off his bike, and never moved after that. There weren't any witnesses. The bus driver didn't see the body until it was too late to stop. No passengers or people on the street saw anything else. The autopsy report said Stein died of head injuries before being hit.

He wasn't wearing a helmet. There were rubber marks along the trolley tracks that matched the bicycle's rubber wheels. His face and arms were covered with scrapes and cuts. There were small chunks of gravel and glass in his mouth and eyes that matched samples from the ground alongside the tracks. I looked at the photos. His face was barely visible; it was mostly cuts.

I had two completely different points of view. The evidence was that John Stein had an accidental death. My feeling was that he was murdered. I had met the boy's mother. I had an instinct about her loss. I knew what I believed.

I sat on a bench by the old trolley station. I looked across at the intersection and felt the slight weight of the police file in my hands. I was looking for a gap between what everyone thought was true and what the truth might actually be. When I am stuck, I have learned to go back to basics. The most basic of these is that people usually see what they're already inclined to see. I thought about how the file in my hands had come to be.

The report was prepared by the police unit called AID, the Accident Investigations Division. Accidents were what they were inclined to see. They were experts at re-creating scenes. They were good at determining from physical evidence, as in this case, exactly where the bicycle hit the track, the speed the bike was going, how far the body went. They were also good at reading medical reports and asking medical questions. They knew no drugs or alcohol were involved, that the victim and the driver had no other medical problems. They would have looked for witnesses, talked to people who lived and worked on the block.

If anyone had thought it was murder, on the other hand, the Homicide Division would have been called in. I was familiar with their routine. Homicide cops look for witnesses in a very different way. They know DAs love witnesses, the strongest evidence they can present to a jury. The homicide cop knocks on a lot more doors than an AID investigator does.

It was a year and a half after the death, but I decided to do what homicide cops would have done. It would take a week, but I didn't have another job. I started that afternoon, working my way up Frankford Avenue, systematically knocking on doors. I didn't tell anyone I was a cop, only that I was looking into a death a year and a half back. They made their own assumptions. I wasn't asked for ID even once. I went three blocks in one direction, then three blocks back the other way. No one had anything helpful to say.

I started at two in the afternoon, and six hours later I was still at it, coming up blank. One old woman who'd been watching led me by the arm out to the sidewalk. She waved her hand, a grand gesture taking in the street and both directions up and down the block.

"You're saying it happened at night, right? Well, mister, look around."

I did what she said.

"See all the gates and bars on the windows and doors? Nobody goes out at night around here, except the whores and junkies."

Old-lady wisdom was better than what I had. I was not going to find my witness from the people who lived in the two-story row houses that lined the street. I had to switch my search to the nights.

CHAPTER THIRTEEN

Over the past week, Rachel Curren had tried to get to seventy pounds on the butterfly. She hadn't managed it yet. She'd seen few men who could lift that much, but she knew she had the strength. The machine, weighted curves like black wings emerging from a straight steel spine, defeated her each and every time, but she kept trying. She had always been a worker, all her life.

She slammed the two half circles back to clear her way off the seat and cursed the machine as she did.

"You hate that thing, don't you," said a young guy, sitting on a bench across from her at the Y. "I've never seen a woman work so hard."

"That's between me and the machine," she said. "Not me and you."

She got up slowly and walked away. At the cooler, she splashed water on her face and used a large white towel to dry her neck. She was tired but she could do more. She was used to being tired; not sleeping well most nights had that effect. Still, she felt good about the condition she was in. She had previously worked with trainers but found they didn't push her enough. Ideally, she needed to be around serious male lifters, so she could compete and compare. But when she worked out in gyms where those types gathered, she found she envied them too much.

Men had a chemical advantage. Their bodies were made to translate lifted weight into muscle, while she was limited by gender to staying relatively lean. Working herself up to a bulk that was essentially male appealed to her. She had gone through phases when she'd tried for such transformation, pushed herself hard enough, spent two to three hours a day with the iron, then run for an hour after that. But her physical identity was too robust. Her breasts and similar areas of stored fat and soft tissue resisted change. She tightened and acquired power but the female form remained.

She had worked out since the age of ten, initially acting from an impulse she didn't understand. At certain moments when she was thoroughly immersed in exercise, in those early years, she felt, at least for a short time, complete. The sense of emptiness and the specific ugly, guilty thoughts that drove her were temporarily removed. The missing pieces of her life were all still dead and gone but the nagging hurt was eased.

In that first year after her parents and brother died, she'd been moved to her aunt's. It was the same town her parents had lived in, only three blocks away. She had not understood why she couldn't stay home. She screamed at her aunt and uncle about that. She believed at first that if she stayed home, her family would return. She gave in because she didn't have the strength, but she wouldn't accept the welcome of her relatives' arms. At night, awake when they were asleep, she made her way down the stairs and out into the street. She stayed out and felt free, but she never ran away.

One of the vows made then was the one she most faithfully pursued, exercising for at least an hour a day from then on, and sometimes far more. Other vows were made as well, each of them also followed through. But the first of her vows, made the first night, was the basis for all the others. She had promised to make herself strong.

As an adult, the obsession continued. She worked out in the late afternoon or early evening throughout the year. She exercised every Saturday and Sunday morning from eight to noon. She went from one part of her routine to another with minimal rest, organized, systematic, intense. In public, she attracted attention. She was aware of the voyeurs, and she had learned to tell the passive from the ones who wanted to get involved. She had tried both women and men as partners in her long workout routines. They usually couldn't keep up.

Without exception, the men she met and slept with loved this aspect of her at first. But her relationships always ended quickly and the same way. She'd be with them, wanting the closeness, and feel something old and familiar building inside her, alongside the desire. It was a coldness that numbed all pleasure and sensation, and left in its wake no feeling.

She studied the file late into the night. The death was a tragedy but also a powerful negligence case; it could win the family millions of dollars. Mary Cooper died because the city allowed the park bridge to deteriorate and didn't take any steps to warn the public of possible dangers.

The file was thick with photographs. Negligence cases were all about arousing sympathy from juries—photos were key. The ones obtained from Mary's family showed an attractive young woman. Police photos of the accident showed an old stone bridge in disrepair and Mary Cooper's body. She wasn't recognizable anymore.

Rachel was still up at five in the morning. She looked out her living room window at the dark street. A familiar feeling came, something she was accustomed to late at night. She felt guilty about the death. She always felt that way about the victims.

She closed her eyes to erase the image of the stone-covered body, to replace it with the smiling woman still alive. But in her mental image she couldn't see the woman's head. She saw thick, slate stone, blood-slick, where the face should have been.

She shook her head and opened her eyes, expecting the sight to disappear as her visions always did. But she still saw stone. She calmed herself, took deep breaths, felt the air-conditioned chill of the window against her hands. She picked up the file again. The woman's family lived in northeast Philadelphia. The families were never hard to find; only the dead disappeared.

She waited well past sunrise, then drove to the Cooper house. There was a curved driveway in front. She stayed in the car and looked in the windows of the large house. She was interested in victim's families, in survivors. She was one herself. She liked being near enough to mourn. She sometimes went to the funerals and stood alone. Each and every time, she relived the funeral of her parents and brother. She had been very brave, they all said, a ten-year-old bearing a tragic loss. Everyone had comforted her. Nothing had helped.

It was almost nine in the morning. She looked at the file. The funeral was scheduled for Jordan's on Monday. There had been a long delay, because it took police more than a week to identify the body. The family had lived through not hearing from their daughter for days, then fearing the worst, then knowing it. Rachel decided to pay an early visit to the Coopers.

They always made funeral parlors look like fancy houses, she thought. The places had long couches and deep chairs, ornate designs and muted colors, oil paintings on the walls. The parlors had cleaning rooms out of sight, like kitchens redirected to new ends for the dead. In their sinks and on their tables, corpses were washed and made up, their appearances altered enough to satisfy the grieving. A black-suited army in the sitting room squeezed memories and forced out tears.

She told the manager she was helping the Coopers pick out Mary's coffin. She followed him to the casket room. Forty or fifty coffins of gleaming colored metals and wood neatly lined four walls in descending order of grandeur and cost.

"You may want to start here." He was young forties, she guessed, hair long in back and bald on top, in a dark blue suit. He stepped ahead and led her to the wall on their right. "These are sturdy and long lasting, airtight once closed, tasteful and dignified inside and out. It's the model most people choose. They're very comforting."

She noticed the polished metal that framed the casket's top, and the soft velvet that lined the interior. At the far end of the room were coffins of plain pine, nearly white. The soft wood looked pale and thin, like cardboard, in contrast to the thick wood and substantial metal of the others.

"They're very comforting," the salesman said again.

He spoke about coffins as if they were for the living. She didn't listen. She said she couldn't make up her mind. She knew she wouldn't have to ask to be left alone. It was part of their salesmanship to leave you there after you had the guided tour.

"Take your time," he said. "Just come out and tell me when you're ready to choose."

She had already selected. She waited for him to leave. When the door was closed she crossed the room to the pine box. It did not have a hinged top like the others, only a panel of thin wood to one side. The inside was as bare as the outside.

The box was on a metal table low enough to give an unimpeded view into its shallow depths. She remembered a vista that mirrored the simple coffin, a wide patch of wild grass grown high, a clearing surrounded by old, thick trees, branches bare in late fall's early chill. She remembered feeling cold, the air white vapor as she took her breaths. In front of her on the ground was the bare pine coffin, top closed. The coffin opened, as if moved by invisible hands. She stepped forward, wanting to see but afraid. She heard a droning voice but no words, only sounds. The top of the coffin slid fully back. She put her hands in front of her face, shielded herself from the unknown. She stiffened and willed herself not to move. The force that opened the coffin moved her forward to its edge. The top fell away. She had to look down into the open box.

She opened her eyes and looked around. Only a minute had passed. The rows of gleaming shells still held empty beds, the mattresses and pillows silk, soft and long. Where are the ones for children? she wondered. The coffin she saw in her visions was a child's.

After her parents and brother died, she had often stayed by the gravesites too long. Her aunt always came to take her back. She was never finished regretting everything she'd done, the swipes at her brother's head, taking things he prized, his tears, her rage. She wandered from her aunt's house at night to the bank of a hillside across the river from her home. Another family had moved in. She watched their forms flick past the windows and imagined them living the life that might have been her own. She looked down at the waters, the reflected moon below. She had not been back to that river for years. She looked again at all the caskets. They were empty, reminders of the real thing. Eventually they'd all be filled. There was always enough death to go around.

CHAPTER FOURTEEN

When I got home, Molly was there, down on all fours, playing with her black Labrador, Katy, the world's friendliest dog. I stood on the slate patio above the grass in my back yard and watched them have a good time. Last year, she and I had shared our lives, including a bed. We'd tried living in my place, then her place, and somehow neither of those arrangements worked out. Breaking up had been a relief for her and the usual loss for me. But Molly and I were still good friends. After Karen's death, she visited me often.

I'd stopped by City Hall that morning. I had a personal question to answer—about Sean. I'd been thinking about the boy since finding the photograph in Karen's drawer. Marriage certificates and birth certificates are kept in different rooms. I visited both. I learned that Sean had been born six months before Karen and Jerry were married. Karen and I were still together nine months before Sean was born. The birth records listed Karen as the mother and the father as unknown.

I'd told Molly about Sean. Maybe that was why she kept coming by. It seemed as if something big might be happening in my life. As an intern at Jefferson Hospital, she didn't have much free time, but this week she actually had a day off.

We were talking casually when Katy went running past us to

the front of the house. She didn't bark, because she rarely does; we imagined she didn't like putting anyone off. The visitor was Sean. He rested his bike against the white wooden fence and came down the path. Katy was at his side but he hardly seemed to notice. Grief works so many different ways.

I braced myself for something—I wasn't sure what. I know it was guilt that made me feel he might ask if I was his father, and if so, why I hadn't acknowledged it for fifteen years. There was no reason he should ask, but the questions were foremost in my mind. It seemed like a long time before he spoke.

"I have some questions."

"Look, Sean—"I started to explain.

He interrupted me. "Did this guy Hartman have anything to do with my mother's death?"

I was relieved he wanted to talk about Hartman.

"Your mother died of cancer," I said, as if that were a gentler way to be killed.

"I know that. I don't mean that," he said, sounding annoyed that I didn't understand. "I mean, did he do anything that made my mom die faster, or that kept her from getting help?"

He wasn't an ordinary kid. I walked down the path behind the house and sat in one of the plain wooden chairs. He followed me and stood close by. Molly was out toward the back of the long, narrow yard, keeping Katy entertained.

"No." I made it as certain as I could. Hartman hadn't killed Karen, but he definitely intended to profit from her death. "Hartman had nothing to do with your mother's death."

"But he ripped my parents off, right?" he said. "Maybe that meant she couldn't afford treatment?"

The direct way he put things startled me. It was a style I preferred myself.

"The answer's still no," I said. "As far as I know, your mother had good treatment."

"I can answer that better," Molly said. I hadn't noticed her walking up.

"Sean, Molly. Molly, Sean," I said. "And she's a doctor, so she knows."

"The answer's definitely no," she said. "People die of the kind of cancer your mother had all the time. Treatment or not."

Sean looked at her but didn't say anything. I wondered whether she reminded him of his mother. They had much in common, some of it appearance, which was no coincidence. They were women I was drawn to, both slim and pretty, brown hair, about the same height. Strong in some of the same ways. But this one lived.

"Sean, what do you want?"

I hardly talked to him during my visits to his house and my connection with him was always minimal. I was friends with his parents, but distant with their kids. I wondered if he knew anything about me other than that I was someone who occasionally did carpentry work with his father. Yet he had gotten my address and come three miles to visit.

"I want to help get him," he said. "I don't know what you plan to do, but I know my dad expects you to do something to Hartman. I want in on that."

He was serious about whatever he had in mind. "What exactly do you think you can help me do?"

"I can do anything we need to do. Believe me, I'm tough enough."

I believed him. He looked something like me in build, a tall, thin kid who was going to be big. But it wasn't my toughness I saw in him. It was hers.

"We don't need tough, not that way. I think Hartman stole money from your father, like you said, and from other families too. And I'm going to get that money back. But not by beating him up."

"How, then?" he asked, as if there were no other way.

"What Hartman did was a crime. But if we go to the police, your family won't get the money you deserve. Instead, I can deal with him, threaten him, tell him if he doesn't pay your dad what he owes, I'll take the evidence to the police. I know he'd rather lose some money than go to jail. That's what I do. But there's nothing much you can do to help me."

He bent down and picked up Katy's tennis ball and tossed it from one hand to the other. The dog was intensely interested; tennis balls were near the top of her list. The boy barely noticed. I had never seen a kid ignore a dog like that, let alone this particular one. Suddenly she lunged, getting the ball in her mouth. He didn't let go. The harder Katy pulled back, the more he resisted. It didn't seem like a game. Molly and I glanced at each other.

"Hey, take it easy," she said. "It's no use now, no one's ever gotten a ball back from Katy that way. Let go for a while and she'll drop it. That's the only way."

He ignored her and kept pulling at the ball. He looked angry.

"Hey, relax," I said. I put my hand on his shoulder.

He shrugged me off. "Ah, she can have it." He let go of the ball and walked over to his bike. "I got to go. Keep the damn ball."

"Wait a minute," I called to him, but he had turned and headed off. I almost went after him but that didn't seem right. I had let go of him for fifteen years. I couldn't change that now.

· · ·

I went back to the Frankford Avenue trolley tracks that night. The intersection looked different close to midnight, dark and empty, a small car-repair shop completely fenced in, a ring of swirled barbed wire above the fence. All of the shops were closed. The car and bus traffic were light, and there were no pedestrians in sight.

I walked two blocks north, to the only area where there were signs of life. An elevated train and its steel posts dominated the landscape. The area under the tracks was run-down. Leaning against the locked gates and metal walls of the closed shops were a half-dozen hookers. They were in a variety of outfits with the common theme being skintight and bare. Their faces were covered with heavy makeup that almost succeeded in making women out of fifteen- and sixteen-year-old girls.

Some men were hanging out in the parking lot of a closed supermarket on the same block. Their near total lack of interest in the girls made clear their true interest, selling drugs. Everyone on the street was white, buyers and sellers. The ones who didn't live there came from the Northeast. Frankford was a major route into town.

None of what I saw was a secret to anyone who lived in the area. Prostitutes and drug dealers in this parking lot were as openly advertised as any well-known stores. I approached one of the girls. She was tall enough to be a woman, but the makeup didn't do much to hide the fact that she was probably about fourteen.

I had once tried to do a story about underage prostitutes in the city. It turned out it couldn't be done. The libel and privacy laws required the newspaper to get their parents' consent to do any story that mentioned their names, described them in detail, or published photos. Almost all of them were runaways. They ran away from their parents. The law didn't recognize the true guardians, their pimps. But a witness to a murder could be underage.

She spotted me coming from a block away. By the time I got close, the short, white, skintight leather skirt had somehow gotten tighter and shorter. It was a hot night; in recognition of it, she was half bare. Her pink blouse was tied halfway up her belly. She had on sandals instead of shoes. It wouldn't have taken her too long to get undressed. It was a cute-little-girl kind of look, worn by a girl. She must have thought the little-girl experience was what I had in mind.

I bet she was a good producer for whoever ran the show. She didn't talk first, because that was the rule. I had to initiate the contact, in case I was a cop. I said hello. That was apparently enough for her to start the routine.

"Looking for company, mister?"

The line hadn't changed since World War II. The word *mister* had the proper sexual spin, childlike and seductive at the same time.

"I want to spend some money, but just for information. I'm looking for anyone who might have seen something on a night about a year and a half ago, when a guy got run over by a bus on Frankford and Torresdale."

"A year and a half ago," she said, as if I'd asked her about another century. "Oh, man." She brushed her thick brown hair back with one hand in a gesture that she couldn't have learned anywhere but the movies. Then she walked away.

"I'll be here the next few nights," I said. "If you know anyone, send 'em my way." I was talking over her shoulder. I couldn't be sure she heard. On the other hand, I was talking about money, so maybe she heard everything I said.

I walked the whole two blocks of the strip. I spoke to eight more girls, none of them old enough to be called a woman yet. By the time I got to the fourth one, I was talking to them in bunches. I was the night's entertainment in between tricks. I didn't bother with the dealers because I'd end up with a truck-load of witnesses so good at lying I wouldn't know who to believe. I told them I wasn't a cop and that no one would have to go to the police. I told the last small gathering that I'd pay five thousand dollars in cash to anyone who saw John Stein the night he died. They were all polite. But I still came up blank. It would take time.

CHAPTER FIFTEEN

It was a wasted day. I couldn't get the image of John Stein's glass-flecked eyes out of my mind. Nothing I thought of doing had much appeal. I had already worked out with free weights for an hour and that hadn't helped, not even a little. During the baseball months of the year, I was once able to lift myself out of funks by going to a game. But now I felt that option was closed.

And this was one of the rare days the Phillies were playing a weekday-afternoon game. When I was a kid, major-league daytime games were routine, almost daily during the summer. These days, once every six weeks was about as often as it got—the so-called "businessman's special." Having daylight and an opportunity to pitch, bat, and field when you could see the ball without a million watts of lighting would never again be enough of a justification for scheduling a ball game.

The reason was television and its deified patron, the dollar. There was no point in playing daytime games without a television audience to watch the beer commercials. It had finally reached a point that the labor disputes, lockouts, and strikes had knocked me off as a major-league fan. Baseball was as close as my family ever had to a religion, but the game and its true believers were a distant second in importance to the interests of the millionaires who now owned and played the game.

I reached across the couch for the papers on which I'd taken notes a few days before. I still had Rachel Curren's number. The line was busy the first few times I dialed. After a while I got through. I reminded her who I was and she turned out not to need reminding. That was a good sign.

"I'm taking advantage of the fact that you work at home," I said. "This isn't work-related in the slightest. I was wondering, since you're your own boss, if you have any time off this afternoon just to get together. I'd like to see you again."

"That depends," she said, "on what you have in mind."

"Doing anything to brighten up the day." Saying things outright was one of the benefits of being single and thirty-eight. She either was or wasn't interested.

"I'm still waiting for details," she said.

"I was thinking Phillies game before I called you. But before you answer, I have to tell you that even if you want to, I can't go. I'm one of those people who will never get over that damned baseball strike."

"Okay, so that's something we can't do," she said. "But how about this: I use the late afternoons to work out. That's still the plan for today. If you want, you can come along. You'd have to work out, though."

"I wouldn't even have to change clothes," I said. "And I've already done my weights, so I hope you don't start with that."

"I usually do, as a matter of fact," she said, "but we don't have to meet for that part. How about a hike in the park? Valley Green. We can meet in the parking lot there at five."

I got to the park shortly before five. She was already there. She looked like a regular hiker, at least by the clothes—khaki shorts and ragg socks, which were the standard issue for this particular activity. And she wore hiking boots that were relatively new yet still looked hard-used. She wore a tank top, which wasn't anything specific to hiking but gave me an unobstructed view of great muscular definition all over. I wasn't sure I'd want to see a woman built any better. Her hair was bundled back, and around her neck was a bandanna, which meant she had some experience dealing with sweat.

I said hello and got a friendly smile and brief hello in return, and then she headed out toward the beginning of the trail, taking it for granted I was following. We weren't in the office, but she was definitely in some other kind of work mode. I hustled to catch up. I had the feeling she was moving quickly into whatever her usual routine was. Judging from the shape of her, it was likely to be intensive. I didn't mind the activity, but it really wasn't the reason I'd called.

"Did you grow up around here?" I asked.

"Nope. Bucks County," she said.

She was close to thirty, one way or another, I was pretty sure. That meant she had grown up in a version of Bucks County that no longer existed, a rural place.

"I know Bucks pretty well," I said. "What part?"

"Springtown," she said, looking at me for signs of recognition.

I didn't give her any. I hadn't heard of Springtown, but what that meant was that she had grown up on a farm, or at least in one of the county's very small towns. I had visited Bucks County a fair amount and knew most of the places of any size. For a long time, I harbored the idea of finding an old house there on some pretty land and rebuilding it myself. In the fifteen years I'd held that idea, the Bucks County I liked had pretty much disappeared to new development.

"I'll bet Springtown was a nice place to grow up," I said. "And a lot different now."

"I wouldn't know," she said. "I haven't been back."

It didn't feel like she was putting me off, but childhood was clearly a time, and place, she had been glad to leave. She liked to defend the powerless. It might have been a taste she acquired a long time ago, I thought.

Talking hadn't slowed her down at all. I increased my own pace and the two of us, side by side now, made our way down into the green and to the beginning of the trail that led into the woods. Doing everything by silent agreement when we weren't following her lead, we headed off the trail and into the uncut wooded hillside. We could have gone across the slope and reconnected with the trail when it plateaued shortly above our heads. But we didn't take the easy way around. Instead, we took off vertically, cutting straight up through a trailless stand of thick, squat maples and reedy oaks. The trees offered security and shelter, curving upward to the sky as they looked for light, angling their branches and leaves. They grew at odd angles from the hillside.

The peak rose straight above us now, and climbing it was sheer rockwalking, digging our fingers into thin layers of hard, spare dirt. We didn't talk because we couldn't. We turned our efforts up a notch. We moved like trains, in steamy jerks, destined upward because that's where the track inside our heads went, pushing our bodies like machines. I felt things happen as they always did when I got to my breaking point during workouts, my strongest runs, the times I did a heavy construction job by myself. I didn't mind the way she pushed us. I needed the challenge.

My senses got sharper, to the point the world was a different place, full of strong visions and sounds. I heard a roar that wasn't inside me, but the sound of cars rolling across the Henry

Avenue Bridge, far above us. I heard in the emptied-out air around us the rush of water from the Wissahickon Creek way below. We were beneath the crest of the hill, the highest point of the park, and we had made it there, strained to extremes. Above us was a narrow plane, and when she reached it she stood there for a moment. I looked at her, the incredible build lined in sweat and dirt, the skin painted strange and golden.

It wasn't a perfect day. The white clouds had some dark in them. In some places, the greenery disappeared completely, replaced by long stretches of pale slate rock faces, bulging stones mounted in the steep dirt. She had the strength to take them with, more than I did. Her arms were perfectly developed. She did the round rocks by reaching to either side and spreading herself out, arms like pincers, capturing the stone as if she were going to lift it, then using the force she generated between her arms to brace herself so she could get her legs up and take a step. I knew exactly how hard that was to do, but it seemed effortless for her.

Whenever we hit a small ledge or flatter piece of wooded ground, I tried to make it base camp, but she kept moving on. I couldn't remember the last time I'd worked as hard. I had the feeling this was routine for her. I kept up but paid the price. When we reached a summit, I was the one making noise moving air, not she.

"So now that I've proved I can keep up with you," I gasped, squatting and replacing some of the fire in my lungs with cooler air, "or that maybe you can totally wipe me out, what's next?"

She smiled but didn't say anything.

"This was a test, right?" I pursued it.

"No," she said. "It's just the kind of exertion I like. Didn't you want to come along?"

She hadn't squatted herself, or done anything that indicated she needed renewal, though I thought I could see her breathing hard. She took a step off the level ground we were on and I felt as if I had only a second before she once again had us moving down the hill at a fast clip.

"Wait," I said. "If we don't sit and rest for a minute, I'm going to cool off by falling down this hill into that creek down there."

I could see she didn't want to, that it meant something to her to slow down. But after hesitating, she seemed to decide it was okay. She was giving me a gift. So we officially stopped climbing for a minute. She stepped over to a gently sloping patch of the hill, with grass and small trees to give us a hold and a place to sit. I moved beside her.

"So tell me more about why we're not at the Phillies," she said.

Maybe we weren't in work mode anymore, I thought. I was glad she gave me that opening. I tried to tell her about baseball, what it meant to me, why it was more than a game.

"My father was a lifetime minor-leaguer, from the time he left high school until a few years before he died. I inherited that territory, as surely as if he passed on to me a family business or estate. He didn't have the talent to make it in the major leagues, but I was definitely headed that way. I played minor-league ball in Reading, just like him. He had prepared me for the game in every way, down to my name: George Herman, after the Babe. I didn't like telling people about that. But other than denying the name, I didn't fight his plan. I worked hard, and I could play. I was a big kid. I had a fielder's range and I could hit. And the better I got, the better my dad's life became.

"Classic father-son," she said. "The Little League parent living through his kid."

"That's right," I said. "Except in this case the league was going to be big. We missed each other at Reading. He was gone from there five years before I arrived. But there were still people there who knew him. One was a guy named Jeff, mid-thirties and, like a lot of other guys, hanging on for one more year. He had no dreams left. Guys who weren't going to make it always hated the ones who were, but Jeff had lived past the hate. We were talking about my father one day and he said something I never forgot. He said that because I was going to the big leagues, my father's life had been redeemed.

"It was an odd word for a guy who made his living playing ball. But I knew what he meant by it right away. My father's plans had never worked out for himself, and now, despite that, everything would be good. Because his world was a place where a lifetime minor-leaguer could make things right if he had a son like me."

She asked me what everyone always does.

"So you made it to the major leagues?"

"No, I never did. I got injured in a game, bad enough that it ended my career. But my dad died just before the injury, so at least he never knew. He got his redemption from something I never even did."

She didn't say anything for a minute. Then she whistled. "It's amazing you still talk about going to games."

"I love baseball," I said. "But I hate it, too."

"Lots of things are like that," she said, as if the configuration of feelings was very familiar. There seemed to be a thought she wanted to share. I wondered what it was she loved and hated, but she didn't go on and I didn't ask. I was conscious of the quiet around us. Then the wind picked up and the noise of the world around us returned. The moment of closeness passed. She stood up, stretching as if she was shaking something off, then turned toward the path. "Come on," she said, without waiting for me to get up. She took off running, as fast as when we started up the hill. Our interval of rest had ended.

CHAPTER SIXTEEN

I knew Hartman only by his victims. I decided to get a closer look at him the next morning. Northeast Philadelphia was where he worked and lived. The area was white and working-class, people who wanted secure lives but didn't have the money. It was a natural terrain for Hartman's kind of scams.

His office was a new three-story building. The entire front was glass; you pushed through big glass doors to get in. Lettering on the brass-and-wood sign said BETHLEHEM CASUALTY & LIFE. I wondered who else worked there and what they knew. The doors were locked at eight in the morning. I didn't see anyone inside.

I waited there until he arrived. He parked a black Cadillac in the spot closest to the entrance. Jerry's description of Hartman was perfect: neat black hair, a bit under six feet tall, trim, square-jaw good looks, a man in his late forties who looked much younger. He went into the building for only a few minutes and then walked out with a briefcase, locking the door behind him. He got back in his car and I followed him to his first stop. It was a high-rise South Philadelphia project. The neighborhood was low-rent, poverty in equal measures for black, white, and brown. He parked in the building's lot and I did too, on the other side. There were other Cadillacs there, but only his was new.

He took the elevator straight to the top, twenty-two. I waited for the next car, chose twenty-one, then walked up a flight. I stood at the stairwell door and listened more than looked down the hall, to keep out of sight. Hartman picked an apartment and knocked. When someone answered, he stayed outside the door while they talked. I snuck glances. When he finished I saw money in his hand. He moved down the corridor a few steps and knocked on another door.

He had a file in hand he checked before each stop. Each contact was the same routine: a few minutes of talk I couldn't make out with a person I couldn't see, and he usually walked away with some cash. He went to eight apartments on the twenty-second floor.

He took the elevator down one and did the door-to-door routine again. I never got to hear all the words. I needed a better way to know what was going on. I guessed he'd be working the building most of the day, so I left. I didn't have to go far, because there was a phone booth outside. I could see Hartman's car. It was a good enough spot.

I called the *Inquirer* and asked for Tyler. I got his voice mail instead. I left a message asking him to call me at the phone booth. If he was out for the day and didn't check his messages, I'd be out of luck. And I was likely to have competition for the phone before long. But I also had nothing to lose.

Fifteen minutes later when the phone rang, I still had the booth. I told Tyler about Hartman and the cash and asked him to make sense of the clues.

"Not a problem," Tyler said. "What he's doing's not illegal, though it should be a crime. It's an old insurance game. Very profitable, really worth his time. What people call ghetto insurance, or funeral insurance. Debit insurance is the industry term. It used to be worked exclusively on blacks in small Southern towns. Now it's in all the big cities, like here, and they hit up anyone who's poor.

"It's usually sold just that way, door to door. The pitch—if you could hear him do it—would go something like: 'These are dangerous times. Your kid might catch a bullet, you might get hit by a bus. Funerals cost a lot. For twenty-five dollars a week, you get a policy to cover that.' Convenient because the agent picks up the cash—in these neighborhoods nobody trusted checks. And it's a savings plan, because if no one dies, you get all the money back after ten years."

I heard the pattern of the pitch in what he said. "Whole life again."

"You got it," Tyler said. "But these are really the worst consumer rip-offs in the business. For a thousand dollars a year, you're buying a five-thousand-dollar policy. That price is unbelievable. Gray, if you paid a thousand a year for term life, you could buy a million-dollar death benefit."

"But for Hartman it's very small sums. What makes it worth the work?"

"Remember the kicker with whole life. The agent gets one hundred percent of all the premium payments for the first year, and a percentage forever after that."

The math of thieves; I worked it out in my head. A couple of hundred worried grandmothers buying ghetto funeral insurance would get Hartman two hundred thousand dollars in a year, to start.

I thanked Tyler and headed back. Hartman's car hadn't moved. He was still working hard. I pushed the elevator button and waited, and when it came I stepped in. Hartman was standing in the cabin, by the door. I didn't get out. The doors closed and the elevator moved up.

I took my close look. He was a few inches shorter but not smaller than me. He was wide—neck, shoulders, and chest. His face was lean. His eyes were small and their color dark blue. I'm not bad at following people. Yet somehow he had spotted me. The elevator continued up.

Hartman neither moved nor spoke. I let the side wall of the elevator take my weight. He reached past me to the controls and pulled out the single red knob. The elevator shook to a halt and moved a little side to side, like a barely suspended cart at the top of a Ferris wheel. It was quiet. In a stopped elevator, that didn't make sense. Unless the alarm was cut.

"Who are you and what do you want?" he asked.

I thought about Karen. I wanted to take him now but I didn't know enough.

"I'll tell you when I'm ready," I said. "Not before."

"People who bother me get hurt. Use your head," he said.

He dropped his hand off the panel, catching a switch on the way. The overhead lights went off. I wouldn't risk fighting him for the lights. I moved quickly to the back wall, the one he'd started on. We were in a black cage and I could see nothing. I eased down the wall into a crouch, following an instinct to be somewhere else.

He tapped his fingers against the side of the metal, a loud staccato beat emerging from the wall, then suddenly stopped. I tried squinting light into the car but nothing erased the dark. The car jerked as he moved where he thought I was. In the noise, I shifted position to the wall where he'd been, getting my legs under me, rising into a crouch. I didn't have his location.

Once I did, I planned to do something about him. I didn't like the game.

His hands were suddenly around my ankles and I couldn't pull free. He yanked up and put me on my back. I couldn't get my arms up, and then he was on my chest. His weight forced me flat. His knees were on my upper arms, his hands on my wrists.

I can't be held that way; my shoulders are too big. I shrugged and moved him off me. I tried to get a knee up into him but missed. I reached for the center of his body, where I thought he was; I only grabbed air. I punched, but rammed my knuckles into the wall. In a small metal box in the dark, he had disappeared.

I scrambled away, into a corner, trying to shrink, but he was behind me as I came up. He jabbed into my neck, held on with one hand, and searched for my windpipe with the other. I tucked my head down into my chest and shoved back fast, my body against his, into the wall.

I caught him but it didn't stop him. He came off the wall, used the momentum to push me fast. I got my arms up in time to keep my face from being pulped. He hit the side of my head with a closed fist. My ear popped as if he'd broken the drum. I brought my elbow back into his side. It had to hurt him but he didn't make a sound. I followed up and again he was gone. He was familiar with this odd terrain. I wondered how often he took people for the ride.

Waiting calmly in the dark wouldn't do enough. But there have been some great hitters who practiced their swings in the dark, imagining pitches, aiming the bat across the ball's invisible path. Hartman was somewhere in the elevator with me. It wasn't that big a space. I put my hands together and swung my arms across the space, then back again as fast, stepping forward after every swing.

I missed until I caught him in the middle with a two-handed fist. I buried my hands deep in his side and heard him make a noise he hadn't planned to make. I hit him again and this time heard him fall back against the wall. Now I could find him and take him. And then the light burst on.

He was bent over, but he was grinning. Seeing his condition and his attitude, I stopped.

"That's enough," he said. "You're good."

I pushed the button in. We started down.

"Now tell me who you are and what you're after." He spoke as if our fighting had created a bond.

"Just a guy you met in an elevator," I said. We hit the bottom and I got out. I liked bothering him. I hoped his failure to learn what I was after shook him up. It was only the beginning.

CHAPTER SEVENTEEN

That night I returned to Frankford Avenue, under the el. It was the fourth night I'd been back. The prostitutes and drug dealers hadn't found some place else to go. But this time someone had made me a date. She looked old enough to have been in the neighborhood for a year or two, if she'd started hooking at the advanced age of sixteen. She had graduated from the little-girl look, styled herself for a man who wanted a woman and was willing to settle for a seventeen-year-old in grown-up clothes. She had on a dress and very high heels.

"I might know someone who saw something," she said. "If I introduce you, what do I get?"

"Why not just tell me it's you and take the whole five thou." Usually when they said it was a friend, I knew, I was already talking to the informant.

She nodded as if she'd decided not to pretend. "Who are you? And why pay so much?"

"First you have to tell me what you saw. Then I'll tell you what it's about. I promise I won't go to the police, and there's nothing you need to do after you tell me. You talk. You get the money. You never see me again. Simple as that."

"Let me see the money."

I reached in my pocket and gave her two hundred dollars. She grabbed it and stuffed it away. "That's just good faith. What you're selling isn't worth anything to anybody else. I made the stake big so I could get this done. But I'm not dumb enough to carry five thousand around. Tell me what you know, I promise you'll get the rest, right here, a few hours from now, or anywhere else you like."

She nodded. "It was really hot, really sticky that night. Things were slow. It was still early, ten or ten-thirty. I went with a guy just down Frankford from here, someone I knew. A half-hour job. When he left, I stayed in the room awhile, just to catch a break. On the second floor, over there." She pointed at one of the buildings that overlooked the corner.

"I was at the window to get some air. I saw a dark-haired guy dragging this other guy, who was out of it, stoned or something. He dragged him with one hand. With his other, he was wheeling a bicycle."

I waited for more, but there wasn't any.

"That's it. That's all I saw. When I went back down, I was on the street a little bit when I heard screeching brakes, but no crash. After that, sirens real soon. Two cop cars come down the street, stop by Torresdale, a couple blocks away. There was no more business after that. It was a real bad night."

It made sense that the men were Hartman and Stein. And Stein wasn't drunk or stoned; the autopsy report said he was sober. Unconscious, on the other hand, would explain things very well. It had to be that Hartman waylaid the kid, killed him, then walked him and his bike to the intersection and put him on the tracks. At night, in that crazy place, a bus making a turn wouldn't have had time to stop.

Now I had something to work with. What the girl observed contradicted the police report. It was enough to suggest a murder. Combined with Hartman's motive, which I could show, it was strong enough to force his hand, to move us toward a deal. If he refused, it was probably enough to get the police to reopen the case. A homicide charge would mean I'd lied to the girl and she'd have to talk. But I'd done worse than that.

CHAPTER EIGHTEEN

I slept into late afternoon the next day. I went out running because it is what I do to think and what I do when I'm tired of thinking too much. And Chestnut Hill, where I live, is great for running. There are soft roads, few people and cars, and an endless choice of century-old well-made houses everywhere you look. I am not a risk taker or a wanderer, despite my occupation. I am a homesteading type. I liked where I lived, and I had it figured so I'd never have to leave. Blackmail had taken care of the mortgage. It had made one part of my life secure.

I was running on Seminole. It is a wide street, asphalt, smooth and dark, thickly cloaked with limbs and leaves from overhanging trees. An occasional car zipped by and disappeared like a horse-drawn carriage weaving through a forest. The slope was gentle but definite. I took deeper breaths as I ran.

I did eight miles. When I got home, I had shaken off the night. I sat on the wooden bench outside my living room window, watched old streetlamps come on in front of all the houses, and waited until the early-evening breeze got me dry. I hadn't yet moved when a white Ford pulled up and Rachel Curren got out. I wondered how she knew I wanted company. Maybe even total strangers knew.

She was wearing jeans and a leather jacket. She looked much younger than thirty. But it wasn't youth that made her striking, it was the combination of beauty and strength. She stopped at the wooden gate.

"I looked you up in the phone book," she said. "We're neighbors, almost. I thought maybe we could get a drink. Too nervy?" She grinned.

"I've got plans. A shower, something to eat, reruns on TV."

She took it as an invitation. She opened the gate and came in. "Just do the shower. I'll wait."

I went in and showered. I changed into jeans and a T-shirt and went back out. She was on the bench, legs crossed, gaze fixed on the huge oak across the street.

"Quiet here," she said. "Pretty. How old's your house?"

"Two hundred twenty years. First on the block. In fact, no block at all back then; it was a carriage house at the back of a big property. When they built the street, they expanded the house, adding the kitchen and the room on top of it. There's a cast-iron stove in there, hasn't been used in a hundred years."

She laughed. "Guess you don't eat much hot food, huh?"

"There's a place up the block and around the corner, makes the best burgers anywhere. And it's also my favorite bar. How's that for a coincidence?"

"Sounds great."

I drove the couple of blocks up to McNally's. If you hadn't been there before, you wouldn't know to go in. It was in the middle of a row of shops, and the front was a dark-green wooden door with a small, barely noticeable, dull brass sign. There were no windows to look inside. But beyond the door was a very friendly bar and grill. We ordered burgers and fried onions to go, then sat at the bar to wait. It was a place you could actually watch a Guinness draft being poured the way the Irish did that kind of thing, where the bartender filled half the glass and walked away. Rachel had either had one before or she was good at waiting for things. When the bartender finally finished the pouring, she picked up her glass and took a long sip. I did the same.

"How come you're alone?" she asked.

"How do you know I am?"

"Well, you're out with me, and you had no hesitation bringing me someplace local. And you just look like it. Also I'm guessing. How'd I do?"

I laughed. "You're right about me being alone. I'm interested in not being alone. I even work at it. For some reason, I usually don't succeed. But I'm not alone at the moment, right?" I smiled at her. She smiled back. I willingly played the flirting game. It felt good to take part in a ritual, not to have to think.

"I was married once," I said. "It lasted three years. She was the one who left. Since then I've been in other relationships. Six months is about how long they last. I don't know why. I used to think my competition was their careers, or the ways they were hurt by other men. My latest theory is that the women I get involved with are too nice. I need someone a little more complicated. Or wicked." I looked at her.

"Maybe you do," she said, picking up the glass and finishing the beer. I still had some of mine. She leaned over and kissed me on the lips. The kiss was gentle but she put her hand on my leg. I had probably never had someone so attractive come on to me so strong. It was a gift I wanted to take. But she wasn't far away enough from John Stein in my mind. It was a geography that mattered.

"Ease up," I said. "I don't want to give the bartender a heart attack. He's a genteel guy."

Charlie fixed the burgers and put them in a bag. I took two

six-packs of Harp from the cooler by the door and put them on the bar, grabbed the bag he put them in and led the way out the green door. It was nine. We got in my car. She rolled down the window and put her arm on the frame. She looked out at a little antique shop, where the small clay houses on display seemed to remind us that our lives were only a matter of scale.

She turned and put her arm across my shoulder like a friend who has something to say. Instead of words she turned her gesture into a kiss. This time I did nothing to discourage her.

At the house, she didn't go in. She stepped to the side onto the stone path to the back.

"Give me the grand tour," she said.

"I can't. We've lost the light."

"Give it to me anyway," she said.

She walked onto the stonework patio in back. The garden was a corridor of grass, thick bushes, and tall trees. Trees were all that marked the border between my neighbors and me; I didn't have a fence.

It was a peaceful place. I took a breath deep enough to feel myself relax as I let it out. She came to me, her body pressed to mine, asking for another kiss. That was fine with me.

When we came inside, she opened two beers and handed me one. She drank much too fast. I tried casual conversation, and she drank more, saying little. She used the beer like an anesthetic, the way people with drinking problems do. She was an odd combination, open in some ways, but also sealed tight.

In the kitchen, I microwaved the burgers. I ate and tried to talk some more. She deflected all questions and conversation and continued to make the beer disappear. She noticed the fireplace.

"Does it work?"

"Sure."

"How about it?" she said.

I stepped out to the dry pile at the side of the house and brought in logs. She made a neat triangular stack of big and small wood as if it was something she really liked to do. I tossed her a box of the strike-anywhere kind and she lit it up.

We watched the flames. As we sat comfortably and close, she finished all the beer. She gradually moved closer, her legs over mine. I didn't follow her lead. After a while, she shook her head. "Come on," she said. "What's the problem?" She was puzzled. Her speech was slurred. She was drunk, and she was with a man she hardly knew, who happened to be me. It wasn't a simple situation.

She got up and picked out the best chair in the house, made of big solid wood with deep cushions. She crawled in and fell asleep. She was lying at an odd angle, but the sixty-year-old oak was tough enough to hold her. I cradled her legs and head, and picked her up. Muscle weighs far more than fat and she was difficult to lift. There wasn't a choice of destination once I got upstairs. The guest room was nothing but boxes and files. The only bed in the house was the one in which I slept. I put her down on the side that wasn't mine.

I stayed up for a while but finally got into the bed. Going to sleep would take some time. Looking at her made it take longer still. The window was open wide, the night air refreshing. She had been asleep an hour, most of which I spent wondering why I had turned away her advances before she passed out.

I always had trouble sleeping anyway. I had long ago given up trying to coax myself into uninterrupted hours of sleep. I usually woke up a short time after going to bed late, and then lay there for a while, put the radio on, and eventually fell asleep again. I kept a small AM-FM nearby, and I'd developed a talent over the years for picking up baseball games from lots of cities late at night. After eleven, you can get Cincinnati really clear, sometimes catching Joe Nuxall's gravelly voice at sign-off: "Rounding third and heading for home." In recent years I'd found myself relating more to the announcers than to the players, because so many announcers had been around for a long time and were doing the job more for the love of the game than for money. I often fell asleep with memories of my earlier life, the one in which my job was very clear: Stop ground balls from getting past me, then take a stick and hit the ball so the other guys couldn't catch it.

This particular night I finally fell asleep without the radio. I had a dream about playing on my Double A team. It was my last game. I was rounding third, digging hard for the plate. I'd been going full speed since I took off from first and I was dead out of wind. I saw the ball coming in on a line to the catcher and I knew I had to turn the speed up one more notch. Five feet from the plate, I dove headfirst and smashed into the catcher's chest. He was a 240-pound rock. I never touched the plate. I could feel my shoulder shred and tear. His knee caught my gut and knocked my breath out. I tried to take a breath. Everything around me was dark. The catcher was on top of me. I tried to shove him up and off but he wouldn't budge. I was suffocating, unable to get any air.

Then I realized I wasn't dreaming. I was awake, in bed, and I still couldn't breathe. My face was covered, a pillow pressed down hard on my head. I pushed up with both hands. I couldn't push it off. I panicked and jerked to one side and slid my head out from under the weight. Rachel was holding the pillow; her face was ashen-white. I grabbed the pillow out of her hands and threw it on the floor.

"What the hell—" I yelled.

She didn't speak or move.

"Jesus, Rachel." I got up and stood over her. I wasn't sure what came next. "What were you doing?"

"I don't know," she said. "I have these fits . . . nightmares . . . since I was a kid." I barely heard her speak. She was in a fog, of alcohol and sleep.

"You could have hurt me!" I said.

"Look, I didn't know what I was doing." Some of her color was coming back. "I'm sorry. I need a drink."

"I need you to tell me what your problem is," I said. I made myself stop yelling. "And the last thing you need is a drink."

She got off the bed and headed for the door. She still had all her clothes on, so she didn't have to do anything in order to leave. I got in her way. She didn't go around me. She stopped, her eyes not meeting mine.

"Let me go," she said.

I wasn't holding her, but I stepped aside. I followed her downstairs. She picked up her pocketbook, and when we reached the door, she went out and I stayed in. I watched her get into her car and drive off. I didn't sleep for the rest of the night.

CHAPTER NINETEEN

By the next evening, I turned my attention back to Hartman. He had warned me not to bother him again, so I decided to continue following him. The more of a threat he perceived me to be, the better our deal would get. It was seven o'clock, an hour after Hartman's agency closed for the day. This time I headed for his house, on Primrose, about four miles from his office. If you were from the Northeast and had any money, this was where you lived. I passed the house and parked a quarter block away. A car was in the driveway. I settled in to wait.

I didn't see Hartman. But a boy rode up the street on a bike and stopped not far away. He didn't notice me. It was Sean. He was looking at Hartman's place.

I got out and walked to his side. He glanced at me with feigned lack of interest, then turned back toward the house. He wasn't looking at me but he spoke.

"Waiting for Hartman?"

"Looks like we both are," I said.

Wherever we were going, we didn't get any further than that. Hartman came out of his front door and headed for the Cadillac in the driveway.

"See you later," I said to the kid and hurried back to my car.

Sean followed me, going to the passenger-side door. I didn't have much time to decide whether to take him with me but more time might not have helped. I leaned over and pulled open the lock. The boy eased in as I started the engine. He was quiet and quick about everything he did, not what I expected from a kid.

Hartman turned left onto Pearson. As we drove along, we were close enough to see him through the back window of his car. He kept looking out the sides left and right. He seemed to be cruising rather than going somewhere. Maybe he was looking for potential customers and when he found some he'd stop and chat. It was the nature of his business. He was a thief whose tools were relationships and conversations.

He pulled into the lot in front of Sportsters, a bar and restaurant at the corner of Roosevelt and Grant. I drove past and parked.

"Wait here for me," I said to Sean, but instead he opened his door. "I mean it. You'll blow it for both of us if you go in with me. I'll come right back out. Just wait." He closed the door.

I went in. It was a big place. I didn't have to be noticed if I stayed by the entrance. A hostess approached, dressed like a cheerleader, short skirt and white V-neck sweater with a big *S*. I told her I was waiting for someone. That allowed me to stand and look. Hartman was half off a stool at the bar, drink in hand, taking sips, talking to the bartender and a few customers nearby.

Soon he got up and approached a table where two couples sat. They invited him to join them but he stood instead, talking as they listened, laughing and looking up. He's a neighborhood celebrity, I thought, a guy people liked. I looked him over as he stood there, trying to see what they saw. For me, the charm wore off when you met him up close. I went back out.

"Big news. He's eating," I reported to Sean.

"So what do we do?" he asked.

The answer to that one is almost always the same. "We wait."

I turned to face him, keeping Hartman's car in my line of sight. The boy opened the glove compartment and reached in. It was crowded with papers and small things stored away. He looked through the mess, not in a hurry, going casually through old bills, insurance cards, and scrawled notes with directions for places I'd recently been. I fought the impulse to stop him. He could have done the same thing while I was inside the restaurant and I'd never have known. He'd waited until now because he wanted me to mind.

"Do you really want to help, or do you just want to act like a kid?"

He hesitated, the papers still in his hand. After a few seconds he put them back and closed the glove compartment. He nodded, then looked at me. "I'm serious," he said.

"If we're working together on this," I said, "you'll have to behave yourself. If you want to know something, ask me. And you're going to have to tell me why you're here. Tell me what you think you want from Hartman."

He ignored my question. "I know you're not a cop," he answered. "I don't know what makes my dad so sure you can fix everything." The boy made a sound that started out as a laugh and became something else. I looked at him more closely. For the first time he didn't look bored or angry. He seemed sad. He sighed, then looked at me. "I want to know more about you," he said. I realized it wasn't only Hartman he was trailing, but me.

"You want to know about me?"

He nodded right away. "That's what I want."

It was the question I'd feared he'd ask. It wasn't the time for that discussion. But I could still give him an honest answer.

"Okay, Sean. I'll tell you. I was once a baseball player, and then a reporter. I lost both those jobs, though I didn't want to. I lost the baseball job because I got injured. And I lost the newspaper job because I did something wrong. It's a little harder to tell you what I do now. I'm like a private detective, but it's not even as clear as that. I try to help people like your father."

"Tell me all of it," the boy said, his voice suddenly hard and angry and demanding, not completely satisfied with what he'd heard. "Tell me what you do that's so secret, what you do that's wrong. That's the part I want to know. I know there's more you're not telling me."

I wondered what it meant to him to know about me, what accounted for the desperation. Could he actually be thinking that I was his father? How would he know? Or was there something else? Either way, I wasn't ready to talk about it. So instead I told him how I worked.

"One way I help people is to make other people do things I need them to, things they don't want to do," I said. "Like forcing Hartman to pay your father the money he owes him. One way to do that is to learn secrets about them, things they don't want anyone to know."

He was staring at me. I knew I hadn't given him enough, certainly from my point of view. At that moment, Hartman came out of the restaurant and went to his car. We stopped talking and started following Hartman again. He took the direction away from his house, a left on Grant, a right on Roosevelt, and he drove along slowly. He'd be at the turnpike soon, the city's north edge. He turned onto Byberry Road instead.

I recognized the scattered buildings of distinctive red brick. It was Philadelphia's version of a haunted house: Byberry State Hospital, closed ten years ago by order of a federal judge, originally built to care for the retarded and mentally ill. The judge had said it was unfit for human habitation, as I recalled the phrase. It was notorious for its rotten buildings, so poorly maintained that patients died on decaying floors. The human side was equally high-risk. Some people had died of beatings, or of exposure, unattended outside on winter nights.

He turned left up one of the old asphalt roads and drove through an open area. He had spotted us. I slowed down. He sped up, took a curve, and disappeared.

"You're losing him, go after him," Sean said.

"You said you just wanted to see him," I said. "So did I. We didn't lose a thing."

I started forward, looked to the sides, headed in the direction Hartman had gone. The Cadillac screeched from a side road right at us. I slammed on the brakes, full weight on the pedal. The car shuddered and stopped. Hartman pulled within inches of my front grille, then shot past and stopped by one of the hospital buildings to my left.

The seat belt was tight against my chest, locked in place from the jolting stop. I pulled at the belt and jabbed at the release control at my side. It didn't come loose until I cursed out loud. My knee hurt; I'd banged it on the steering wheel when we stopped. My body made the shift from frightened to angry. I stared at Hartman and opened my door.

Hartman looked back, opened his own door, and stepped out. He walked casually a few steps to the worn gray metal door that was the side entrance to the building. It opened immediately and he went in. I calmed myself down. I had no intention of going after him; I wasn't alone. Then I glanced at the passenger seat. Sean wasn't there. He was over by the building.

I didn't bother calling out. The boy wouldn't listen; he'd

already made up his mind. I ran to the entrance and followed them into the building. On the other side was a square, dark room with enough light from a windowed corridor for me to see and be seen. No sign of Hartman, and the boy was gone.

I had to find Sean. Every shadowed thing became him until I focused better and the objects disappeared. I realized I was standing in a lobby, a once-grand entry hall with a high ceiling and a wide stairway at its center. I pictured worried families greeting institutionalized relatives, with doctors and attendants playing host. Lousy places put their money into lobbies. People rarely looked at back rooms.

I tried yelling and got nothing back. I heard movement upstairs. I ran up. The second floor was a long row of rooms. This was the real place, not the lobby face. I passed rows of identical square spaces, placed next to each other for the ease the arrangement offered guards. Rusted steel bed frames remained where they had been for years, soldered to metal in the floor. Nearby was unmovable metal furniture of the same kind. The beds had metal rings at the sides—shackles, really.

I saw Hartman and Sean at the same time, across from me, on the other side of the landing around the stairs. Hartman was going out the far-side hallway door, wherever it led. Sean was running after him, not close enough to reach him before he disappeared.

"Get him," the kid yelled across to me, as if we were playing the kind of game in which catching someone means you beat him for good.

This *was* a game, I thought. It started when he'd scared us with his car. I wondered what it was about this building, why he was running away from a kid and why he was still in sight. I saw Sean running toward the darkened door. And the second before Hartman went through, he looked at me as he had when we were outside.

"Sean, stop!" I said it as loud as I could, wishing my voice alone could make him freeze. He kept moving. I ran hard his way. I got to the door moments after he went through. When I reached it, I heard him scream.

I stepped through quickly and almost took a twenty-foot drop. On the other side of the door, the room had been ripped away. I had reached back as I fell and caught the edge of what remained of the floor. It was a foot-wide ledge to the left, easy to stay on if you knew it was there; Hartman had undoubtedly used it to walk away. Below where the floor and ceiling had been were metal support beams, jagged metal edges pointing up like huge knives.

I spotted Sean. He had fallen onto one of the rods. The back of his wool coat was caught on the edge. He'd either managed to save himself or simply had great luck. I couldn't tell if he was hurt. I called to him, "Don't move."

I pulled myself up, glanced around for Hartman, then found the stairs to the room below. I ran down the stairs and into the room. Sean was above me, high enough that I couldn't reach him, but not too high if I could get him to fall.

"Right below you, Sean," I said, keeping it calm and soft. "Just get out of the coat, if you can. You'll be okay."

He couldn't see me, but I saw him nod. In the car, I'd asked him not to act like such a kid. I'd been fooling myself. He didn't need any growing up. I watched his movements, trying to time the impact. I braced for him, and then he came, yelling all the way into my arms. It was tough weight to take. It tore at my muscles and brought me to my knees, but I kept him from the cement floor.

"You all right?" I held him.

He looked up. I followed his gaze. His coat was still swinging on the makeshift hook above. I expected to see Hartman, but he wasn't there. He couldn't have set this up for me or the kid, I thought. He had no way of knowing we'd be coming here tonight. This was a place he'd planned a murder, for someone else.

CHAPTER TWENTY

I was out of the Northeast at high speed and back on Bethlehem Pike before I could think much at all. The priority was getting Sean home. He was silent the whole way. I had screwed up by allowing him to be with me when I followed Hartman. I pulled over to the side.

"Tell me how you are. Really."

"Okay," he said, "okay."

When people said it twice, it usually wasn't true. He was reassuring himself.

"I'm taking you home. We've got to tell your dad what happened."

"No! We're not telling him nothing about it."

"Why not?"

"Because then what you do ends. My dad will go after him. And you already said that can't work."

I looked him over. What had occurred was more or less a miracle. No marks. All he'd lost was his coat.

If Jerry knew what Hartman had done, the only acceptable options would be going to the police or going after Hartman, with or without me. I'd have to stop him or do it with him. I had to be cold, the way his own son was being. If Jerry went after Hartman, he'd probably get himself killed. If I went with him, I'd be forced into weak positions to protect him, as I was with Sean today. If Jerry went to the police, Hartman would win. We couldn't prove that Hartman had done anything wrong. After all, we had been following him; he would say he was trying to get away from us.

"All right," I said to Sean. "Your way."

I pulled the car onto the road. He put his head back on the seat, satisfied or drained. He was hard to read. In a few minutes we were at Jerry's house. I didn't even think about getting out. It was Sean's play. He didn't say goodbye when he left.

As I drove off, I thought about his mother, the one who got away. I thought about our last day together.

She had called and said we had to talk. It was a morning after we made love in the park. We sat in her living room on the couch. By then, I'd been to her place a dozen times. All the times before had been good ones. We only had extremes.

She told me it was over. I heard it, but I didn't believe. It got worse after that; she made it make sense.

"You take risks." She said it in the tone she used with clients. It was a fact, the tone said, a starting point, something we were going to face. "You make meaning of your life by going after people no one sane wants to be anywhere near. It's for good reason, but like a lot of good causes it's still a war. I don't want to fight—not with anyone if I can help it. Having a family is what's important to me. So tell me if you're willing to give up what you do, for love."

I wanted more time with her, even a week or a couple of days. I knew what to say to make that happen. But I never did.

She nodded as if I'd spoken. "I'm not just doing this for me," she said. "All my life I've made sure to look ahead. It's more than making plans or lists of things to do. I see down the road, and then I don't lie to myself about it. I see I'm going to have kids. So I'm speaking for them too."

In her mind, we couldn't go anywhere. She saw its end already. I wondered if it would have changed things if that clear, look-ahead vision of hers had been able to see her own early death. But that was unfair, to her and to me. She was great at making decisions. She made a tough one, and she was right. Given the family she made from that choice, I had to say it was a good one, even though she didn't choose me.

I never came up with the lie, simple as that. We sat on her couch and held each other. We cried. And then I left. That's how she got away.

The only way to make it come out all right was getting Hartman into his cage. The more I thought about it, though, the more odd it seemed that no one had managed the deed already. The things Hartman did were so open, so glaringly obvious to anyone who cared to look. He made contracts with people, took their money for years, promised them services and money in return, and then simply refused to pay. He had also arranged at least one murder.

But Hartman couldn't function alone. The insurance company was part of his schemes, and powerful as it was, it didn't seem to know or care what was being done in its name. To support him, the company didn't have to do anything other than its legal business. No special involvement was required.

I returned to City Hall the next day and started at the office of the Clerk of Common Pleas. There were scores of big black vinyl binders holding a decade's worth of alphabetized criminal charges. There was nothing under James Hartman's name.

The civil-court record room was down the hall. I looked under Hartman's name to see if he'd ever been sued. I found six suits over the past eleven years. Six in a decade spoke well for

Hartman's ability to select customers. Even legitimate businesses got sued more often than that. I asked a clerk to pull the files.

In all six cases Hartman was sued for failure to pay a death benefit. He settled out of court five times. The unpaid benefits were one hundred thousand to three hundred thousand dollars; he settled them for twenty-five thousand each. He hadn't been able to keep the families from filing suit, but he did all right in the end. He took them for more than he paid.

The sixth case was different. The file was thicker than the others, full of documents. I read it through. A woman named Ellen Loftus had sued, been offered the usual twenty-five thousand to settle a three-hundred-thousand-dollar-claim on her husband's death, and turned Hartman down. He upped the offer to fifty. Mrs. Loftus still turned it down. The woman wanted the full amount, nothing less. Apparently Hartman had his limits; he refused to pay. The case had gone to trial nine years ago.

The way I read the transcript, Mrs. Loftus had a convincing case. Hartman said the family missed many of the premium payments, and that Mr. Loftus had borrowed against the equity in the account. But Mrs. Loftus hired an investigator and an accountant, and they produced bank records of every payment—no payments had been missed. Then her lawyer had filed discovery motions, gotten access to Hartman's bank records, and showed that Mr. Loftus had never taken any loans. It seemed clear that Hartman had no chance to win the case.

But the jury never got to decide. The judge sent them out and met with the lawyers in chambers, the transcript said. Then he came out and directed a verdict in Hartman's favor, sending the jury home. End of case. The woman's lawyer recorded his objection to the judge's dismissal but never filed an appeal. It seemed certain the judge had taken a payoff to rule Hartman's way and then made a deal with Mrs. Loftus's lawyer. He might have given him cash or promised him future assignments from his court. In Philadelphia, when a judge took a bribe the case was called a blowout. It was not a rare occurrence; the lawyers on both sides did well for themselves and the victim was the only loser in the case. I added Mrs. Loftus to my list of people Hartman would pay back.

The judge's name was Ronald Dickson. I decided to pull all his cases. It wasn't hard to do. You can get a printout of every case a judge hears for any period of time you want. You have to pay for the computer time to run the program and get the list. I asked the clerk for all of Dickson's cases in the past ten years. If any of them involved issues of life insurance, I could check for Hartman's name.

It took time for the clerk to get logged on. It was a two-hour wait to get the printout.

"That'll be a hundred twenty bucks," the clerk eventually said.

I wrote a check to the City of Philadelphia. He scribbled a bunch of numbers on the back of the check and gave me the printout. It was longer than I expected. Dickson had presided over hundreds of cases in the past ten years. The printout had the names of plaintiffs, defendants, and lawyers, and a summary of the cause of the suit and the disposition of the case. Insurance cases were common. There were liability, homeowner's, auto, worker's compensation, and malpractice suits. Most of the cases resulted from car, bus, or train accidents. The city itself was the most frequent target of the suits. Public transportation was a major Philadelphia predator, if Dickson's list of cases was any kind of clue.

The majority of the findings were in favor of the plaintiff, typically for ten to twenty thousand dollars, occasionally for much more. There were several verdicts for a few hundred thousand each. And four people over the decade had received verdicts over a million. I didn't see a pattern. Mrs. Loftus's was the only life insurance case Dickson heard.

The more I learned, the more it struck me how immune to consequences Hartman had been. The scams he ran were blatant frauds. He took money from people by virtue of lies, and told many more lies so he didn't ever have to give the money back. But his immunity also made sense. Prosecutors will usually not go after white-collar crime when it is a matter of one individual stealing from only a few and if they believe the victims can get significant relief in civil court. The guiding philosophy prosecutors used was that justice is often a matter of business, of collecting fines and parceling out the available funds. It was the reason why all the crime on Wall Street rarely stopped. It was the reason the very rich usually came out all right, no matter what they did.

In that sense, courts and the system they were part of were often nothing more than a big probate office, a place with clerical responsibility for adding up and keeping track of assets, and clarifying the distribution of funds. The ordinary words people used to describe their hopes were empty when judges were not particularly concerned about justice.

Something interesting had happened in Ronald Dickson's courtroom; Hartman was involved. I wasn't counting on justice, but I decided to see the judge.

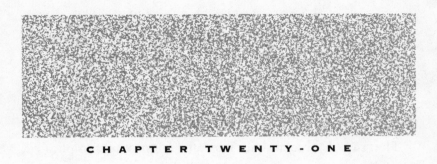

CHAPTER TWENTY-ONE

Judge Dickson's courtroom was not ornate or ceremonial. It wasn't really a courtroom at all. The civil courts in Philadelphia are actually a row of rooms on the middle floors of an ordinary downtown office building. Above and below are accounting firms, mail-order businesses, frozen-food distributors, and hair-replacement companies. It hadn't always been like that. Years ago, all of the city's courtrooms were in City Hall. But as Philadelphia's population increased, so did the crime; even more than that, civil litigation soared.

The rise in civil cases was, at least in part, because Philadelphia courts had a well-deserved reputation for delivering some of the largest monetary verdicts in the nation. Lawyers all over Pennsylvania and New Jersey tried to get their civil cases heard in the Philadelphia court system, even if their clients or the defendants didn't live or work in Philadelphia. The result was that the courthouse at City Hall became too small for the volume of cases brought, and the city was forced to rent space in a nearby skyscraper and turn offices into courtrooms. The converted rooms had jury boxes and witness stands, a bench for the judge, and an area with spectator seating.

I'd been sitting in the back of Dickson's courtroom for hours. He ran the proceedings with a strong hand and an obvious command of the rituals of law and court. He also had the appearance of power—a deeply tanned and lean face, gray eyes, silver hair, and an energetic demeanor. He was more skilled and better prepared than most of the lawyers. And he had strong opinions, freely shared. Judges who often interrupted testimony by witnesses or stopped questioning by lawyers were known as "active." In Dickson's case, the term was too mild.

The case I observed in late afternoon was complicated, involving a labor contract and worker's compensation. After a while, Dickson declared himself "tired" of the extended questioning by lawyers for both sides. He took over questioning all of the witnesses and quickly got to the heart of the matter. He came up with a compromise solution neither side loved but both sides accepted. The lawyers looked embarrassed.

I came back the next day. The first case was a civil suit by a young woman against the city. Her complaint was sexual harassment. She said that police stopped her car in a random check for drugs, and kept her in the back of their patrol car for almost an hour, where the two male officers took turns "patting her down," supposedly to look for drugs.

When the police testified, their attorney asked easy questions and got predictable answers. The cops said the woman was foul-mouthed and aggressive, and they only touched her to restrain her. Then Dickson took over the questioning. He asked one of the cops why he hadn't called for backup, why he hadn't charged the woman with assault, and why he hadn't taken her in. The cop was unable to answer any of the questions well enough. Dickson turned to the police attorney and suggested that he ask for an adjournment so the two sides could settle the case.

It was late afternoon. I stayed for one more case, a suit by tenants against a landlord in a poor section of West Philadelphia. Their claim was that the landlord neglected the buildings. The tenant's chief witness was a thin black woman who looked about fifty. She walked to the stand as if she was in a hurry to get there but sat down carefully and slowly. She testified for half an hour about the rotten conditions in the buildings. She had a good eye for detail and vivid recall. When her lawyer sat down, Dickson leaned over toward the woman and spoke.

"The problem is you people don't take care of the buildings," he said.

The woman stared at the judge. He peered back. Neither of the lawyers moved or spoke.

I had heard cops and prosecutors make similar comments in private. It didn't surprise me that a Philadelphia judge had racist beliefs. Showing it in open court surprised me. He must have felt very comfortable doing anything he wanted in his courtroom.

The woman stood up. Her mouth was open but she didn't speak. I thought she might give the judge a dressing down, but she must have decided that wasn't the way to go. She turned to her lawyer instead. "How can a man like him be a judge in this day and age?"

Her lawyer stepped forward, palm out, gesturing for her to keep quiet. "Please, Mrs. Nole." It was the only thing he said.

I took notes the whole time. Taking notes, literally or not, was an old reporter's habit. I recalled things people said and did, however uncomfortable that was for them and sometimes for me. My ex-wife said it was one of the things about me that bothered her the most. I always seemed to have a mental transcript of what we'd said and did. I always won our arguments. Which was bad, because I lost the marriage.

My note taking attracted the judge's attention. I knew why.

There were only a few judicial taboos. Most of them have to do with language. Cursing is unacceptable. So is making racial comments. Reporters learn to take careful notes in court because judges' stenographers sometimes omit words from their records that embarrass their judge. Witnesses might swear they heard a judge say something, but if the judge denied it, the transcript would probably support him. A reporter taking notes, however—and Dickson probably thought I was a reporter—was a problem.

The judge gestured to one of the court officers, then leaned over the bench and whispered to him. The officer walked past the wooden fence that separated the front of the court from the spectator seats. He came directly to me.

"Can I have a word with you out in the hallway?" he said, gesturing toward the back. He was very polite.

Leaving a place with police, any kind, is tantamount to admitting you are guilty. But I wasn't the one who had done something wrong.

"Tell me right here. I'm listening."

He looked toward the judge. Dickson motioned me to the bench. I walked over. Conversation with the judge would mean looking up a long way.

"Who are you and what are you doing here?" he asked.

"I'm a private citizen in a public courtroom," I said. "What's the problem?"

"You've been here a long time, taking notes. Are you a reporter?"

"No, sir."

"Then why are you taking notes?"

I knew what I was risking in taking him on, but I needed to see how far he'd go.

"I want to make sure I remember details. For instance, you said, '*You people* don't take care of the buildings.' I think a comment like that coming from a judge is an important thing to remember."

"I never said that," the judge said. "Your notes are incorrect."

"Those were your exact words. It's in my notes."

"What's your name?"

"Gray."

He looked me over, carefully, as if he were examining evidence. I wondered what he thought.

"Who do you work for?" he asked.

"Myself," I said.

"Let me see your investigator's license," Dickson said.

"I'm not a private investigator," I said. "I'm a private citizen, I told you that."

"I've had enough of your games," the judge said. "It's clear that you're contemptuous of this court, whatever it is you're doing. I'm citing you for contempt right now. And sending you to jail." He turned to the court officers. "Take this man out of here," Dickson said. "Have the sheriff take him to the Roundhouse."

The officers put me in handcuffs. Then they took me away.

CHAPTER TWENTY-TWO

They call it the Tank. It's a holding cell in the basement of Philadelphia's police headquarters, the Roundhouse. There were twenty-five men in there when the cop unlocked the gate and watched me walk in.

It was a big cell. There was enough room for twenty-five more. Some of the guys were lying on the solid-steel bench, sleeping or fallen over in some sort of daze. Others stood and stared at the green-tile walls. A few paced. The pacers sometimes got close enough to other men to elicit angry looks. Almost all of the men looked run-down, dirty, drugged, or crazed. They were black, white, Hispanic, Asian, and whatever else the world had to offer a basement lockup six blocks from the Liberty Bell. Only one guy was white and middle-class from Chestnut Hill. That was me. So every conscious person in the room was checking me out.

Three sides of the cell were ringed by the steel bench bolted to the floor. It was the roughest sort of seat, a seat the way a punched-out hole in a wall was a window. I looked around. Way up above on the high ceiling was the source of the dim cell light, four bulbs in insets covered by bars. Like the people, they were caged in.

I had used my one call to leave a message for Tyler. I was sure he'd get me out but I didn't know when. It wouldn't be easy or automatic. Dickson would have to agree to let me out; there is no bail for contempt. I knew too much about jails to think my time would pass uneventfully. I found an empty spot on the bench.

Everyone in the cell but me was wearing jeans and basketball shoes, T-shirts, and baseball hats. They were as uniformed as the cops in the offices upstairs. If the people in the cell were uniformed, then I was from a different gang, the kind that wore slacks and shirts with button-down collars. And the gang I was from had a lot more power. We were the guys who could do in whole neighborhoods, and hurt people all the nasty, long-term ways. I was willing to bet most of the other guys in the cell never had the high-level prestigious kinds of jobs that men in suits did—jobs where you could lay off two thousand people so corporate profits could increase by five percent. Or move entire businesses from America to Asia, where people would work twelve hours a day for ten dollars a month. Of course, I'd done my best over the years to not participate in the gang I was part of. But membership was a birthright; I was in the gang for life.

All reporters heard stories about the Tank. The moral of the stories was the harm that resulted from official indifference and the violence of caged-up guys. Middle-class guys who ended up here were sometimes beaten and raped. Detainees with diabetes had died because police wouldn't get them their medication. Escape wasn't an option. I wasn't sure what was.

Some men got up and came toward me. The one out front was fairly short, but reminded me of the old Phillies and Mets centerfielder Lenny Dykstra, who they used to call Nails because he was short and tough. Fighting him wasn't appealing. If I beat him—and it wasn't going to be effortless—I'd have dropped the number of possible opponents from twenty-five to twenty-four. There had to be a better way.

I got up to give myself some room. Shorty stepped up, blocking my way. There was no more than two feet between my face and his.

"What's your nickname?" I asked.

"Up yours, man," he said.

I hit him as hard as I could in the middle of his face. I missed his expression because my fist blocked out his face. But I think he was probably surprised. Being white and from the suburbs and able to fight was deceptive and hardly seemed fair. Not only could I get a cushy job with a decent salary, I could throw a punch. Shorty went down. A tall guy stepped up. I was still searching for an alternative to fighting them all.

I knew the Tank had a pecking order. Every place did. I needed to get the attention of the top guy. The tall guy threw a punch, a loping, ropy, muscled thrust to my left, meant to turn me in that direction so he could do something nasty to the other side of my face. That was a mistake; I couldn't be faked. Years working the hot corner had taught me not to commit to any one direction when a bullet ground ball was coming my way. The third-base greats, like Robinson and Schmidt, did it on instinct and talent. In my case, I did it by learning to slow things down, to not react right away, to think before I moved. I knew if not for that damn injury I'd have been one hell of a third-baseman in the major leagues. The tall guy had never seen me play.

I ignored the punch and grabbed him under the arms before he could throw the next. He wasn't ready for that, and I used my weight to throw him back against the wall. His shoulders hit hard and his neck snapped back like a whip. His head followed. The crack was loud in the silent room. I had now punched out two tickets of admission to meet the king of the hill. I hoped it was enough, because it was either contend with him or contend with everyone. I looked around.

A guy stepped forward from the shadows. He was big, of course. He had a few inches on me, which made him about six-six. He was thick all over, in a way I associated with long-term prison stays. I turned to face him. No one got between us or near us. The tall guy was keeled over. The short guy stirred and sat up but otherwise stayed where he was. I had what I wanted, a shot at surviving by fighting one guy.

He came at me in a straight line. Everyone in the cell moved to the walls as if a wind had whipped them out of the way. I wasn't strong enough to go blow for blow. If we went at it hand to hand, I'd be lucky to come out of it with bruises that healed. I knew there had been deaths in the Tank.

He hit me in the chest with one palm out and I went stumbling back. I turned to the side so he couldn't get at me that way again. He was on me in a second, grabbing with both hands. I broke his grip but it didn't buy me much relief. He went for my neck, and when I grabbed his hand to stop him, he punched me in the face. Nothing he did was a surprise, but he was too strong and fast. Punching wouldn't do it; I'd leave myself open if I tried. I grabbed him hard around the waist. He picked me up and dropped me on the floor. I got my arms down to take the blow but my shoulder hit the stone floor hard.

He kicked me in the stomach. I saw it coming and scrambled back, but it still knocked all the air out of me and hurt like hell. He kicked me in the head, just above my ear. I rang like a bell, but everything still worked. I saw the next blow in time to make him miss. I grabbed his legs and pulled. He smacked onto the floor but kicked me a second after that. The tip of his boot caught me in the chin. I felt blood flow.

The noise level in the room rose. The fans were getting a one-sided fight. I got up and backed away. I took more blows to my body and my face. It wasn't until I looked down that I realized I had thrown up.

He pushed me hard. I went flying back against the bars. I was almost out, but I still had a plan. I needed him to kick me again to make it work.

"Nice boots," I said, more spit than talk.

He laughed. "Wanna try them on for size?"

He aimed it at my crotch. My best move was always to my left on a hard ground ball. I saw it coming and moved. I felt air rush as the kick went by. His leg ended up between two bars, outside the cell. I reached through the bars and grabbed his boot. I twisted and pulled his leg hard against the poles. He groaned and fell to the cement. I aimed my foot at his knee, all my weight behind the blow. I fell on him and held him tight until the bones in his leg began to snap. He grunted, then cursed, then screamed.

I managed to stand up straight. I tried not to walk as badly as I felt. I looked around. Nobody moved. A guy was standing near enough to me to be of use. I grabbed him by the sleeve of his shirt. He didn't pull away.

"Call the fucking cop," I said.

He put his face to the grate nearest the guard station and yelled. No one else in the cell made noise and guy kept yelling until we heard steps. An uninterested voice said, "What do you want?"

"There was a fight."

The cop came over. "I can see that." He looked at me and then at the guy on the floor with the broken leg. He didn't say anything else but he didn't go away either. "I'll get someone," he finally said, and he left.

A few minutes later, three cops came back, entered the cell and took the guy on the floor away. "What about you?" one turned to me and said. I shook my head no. I was safe in the cell now. And I had more plans to make. An uneventful hour later, they came back. Tyler hadn't managed it. But James Hartman came to get me out.

"You look like crap," Hartman said, as we walked out the back door of the Roundhouse.

"I guess you make Eagle Scout now," I said.

"I don't do things for charity. I got you out because it was a chance to get you to listen."

I nodded. "I'm listening."

"You're after me for some reason. And I go after people who bother me. So that's what the elevator and Byberry were about. But all I'm aggressive about is business, nothing else. Whatever you think I did, I didn't do. I want to get you to change your mind."

I didn't really listen to anything he said. "How'd you find me here?"

"Not hard considering you identified yourself to the judge. He called me, of course. Be glad he did. He agreed to drop the contempt charge."

"Okay, I'm glad. But it doesn't matter. You and the judge are getting stopped."

Hartman sighed. He stopped walking and faced me.

"Not me, not the judge. Stuff went on, I know. But it wasn't me, or him. It's someone else you should be after. You might not want to hear it right now, but when you do, come to my office. Meanwhile, leave me alone."

I was free and on the street. My rescuer walked off.

CHAPTER TWENTY-THREE

I woke up at seven in the evening. My head ached and I needed a very large meal. I put frozen food in the microwave and took a long shower while it defrosted and cooked. I ached from the fight in the jail. According to my mirror, I looked the way I felt—awful.

Judge Dickson's ties with Hartman were one explanation of what had happened to me in court and in jail. But there was another possibility I didn't like. Other than Jerry, only Rachel knew I was looking into the insurance scam. Rachel had problems, no doubt about that. But my gut told me her problems were personal and emotional, not criminal. Still, she was a lawyer. She might know Judge Dickson. Would she have had any reason to tell him about me? I'd have to learn more about her. I'd be able to get some of what I needed the usual, reliable way. I went out for a long walk. Doing that and eating was all I could handle. I went back to sleep at nine.

The next morning I returned to the civil-court record room and asked the clerk for all of Rachel Curren's cases. When I finally got the list, it was short. She'd been a lawyer for only five years and had not handled many cases, only thirty-three.

Most of her lawsuits were minor, slip-and-falls. A handful were medical malpractice, none on a large scale. Five of her cases were wrongful death. Those tended to be big deals. I wasn't an expert in civil negligence law, but it seemed to me that five was a large number of major cases for someone who'd been practicing for such a short time.

A quick glance at the printout showed me exactly how big those cases were. Three had already reached verdicts: Two million dollars, three point three million, and five million. One-third of that money was the lawyer's contingency fee. She didn't look like a millionaire, but she was one.

It was a myth that great lawyers can win cases on weak grounds. Most cases were won because the cases had the right characteristics to win. Luck might bring one case like that to a lawyer so young. For five strong cases, she had to have connections. To win five big cases, no matter how strong they were, she had to have help.

I pulled the five case files. One of them was John Stein's. The other four certainly seemed sure things. A twenty-six-year-old carpenter had died from a fifteen-story fall off a construction site in Center City. A twenty-four-year-old mechanic had been crushed to death by heavy machinery at the South Philadelphia navy shipyard. There was a twenty-five-year-old woman blown off a train station platform by a wind gust and run over by an Amtrak train.

They were big-money lawsuits primarily because the victims were young and had big future earning potential when they died. The one besides Stein's that hadn't gone to trial involved a twenty-seven-year-old woman who died in a fire in a new townhouse apartment; there had been a gas leak. The deep pockets for that one might be the city, the gas company, or the landlords, if they were big enough.

I was looking for patterns. It was more about persistence and methodical pursuit than luck. I took everything I knew, whether it seemed related or not, and laid it out. Rachel and Hartman had the Steins in common. I could check if that was true for any other case. I ran downstairs to probate court and went through the index file for the names of Rachel's other wrongful deaths. They came up blank; no probated wills or assets, therefore no life insurance complaints.

The records of the dead were no help. I turned to the living. I had the names and addresses of all four families. Perhaps, like the Steins, the other families had bought fraudulent life insurance policies from Hartman. I went to the corridor and used the pay phone.

"I'm an associate of Jim Hartman, with Bethlehem Casualty and Life," I said. "We need to update a few facts in your life insurance file. Do you have a minute?"

Someone was home at three of the four numbers I called. Everyone I spoke to was courteous and friendly. All four families had insurance with Bethlehem Casualty & Life. They all knew Hartman personally and asked why I was calling instead of Jim. They readily accepted my explanation about how busy Jim had been. I asked about new addresses, births, marriages, and their policy numbers. They were all happy to comply. Two people asked me to say hello to Jim.

I called the downtown tower office of Bethlehem Casualty & Life. The result was not the same as it had been for Jerry. These policies were real, still active, not frauds. But there was a real connection between Rachel and Hartman: The families in all five of her wrongful-death cases had insurance policies sold by Hartman. I knew someone who might willingly tell me more about Rachel's connection with Hartman. I called up Mrs. Stein.

"I'm sorry to bother you again," I said. "I have another question. After your son died, what made you decide to sue the city?"

"Oh, that really wasn't something I felt comfortable doing. It was Mr. Hartman's idea."

"Mr. Hartman?"

"Yes. He told me that what happened to Johnny was really the city's fault—that if the city had done its job and maintained that street properly, Johnny would still be alive. Do you think I did the wrong thing? I never sued anyone before."

"I think Mr. Hartman gave you good advice," I said. "I'm sure he's right—the accident wasn't Johnny's fault. Just one more thing. How did you pick your lawyer, Rachel Curren?"

"Mr. Hartman gave me her name. I don't know any other lawyers. He said Miss Curren was very good."

"She is very good," I said.

I called the Philadelphia Bar Association. I told the woman who answered that my firm was considering Rachel Curren as a staff counsel and I was doing a routine background check. I only needed three pieces of information, all of which the woman was able to provide. When I hung up I knew what college she had attended, the law school that gave her a degree, and the judge she had clerked for. Judge Dickson. The three of them—Rachel, Hartman, and Dickson—were connected. Exactly how, I didn't know. But the worst case might be true: All of the deaths could have been murders staged to look like accidents.

But if I convinced the police and courts that the deaths were murders, another injustice would result. The government agencies and large companies that lost the cases would go back to court and argue successfully that they were not, in fact, liable for the deaths. The victims' families would have to give back the money Rachel had won for them in court.

So I wasn't looking to bring criminal charges—at least not yet. I had to make a deal first, one that stopped the killing and got all of Hartman's defrauded families their money back. To do that, I needed to convince Hartman the murders had been discovered and could be proved in court. I would have to have evidence Hartman wouldn't want a district attorney to see.

Each of the cases had already been investigated by the police and medical examiners. Three of the cases had been to court, the evidence discussed and examined there. The official finding was that each was an accidental death. I doubted I'd find any evidence to prove otherwise, no matter how much legwork I did. I'd have to bluff.

CHAPTER TWENTY-FOUR

I waited for Molly on her porch. She got home at eight-thirty. Her version of making dinner was microwaving supermarket lasagna and opening two cans of peas for the healthy part of the meal. Unlike Molly, I liked to cook. The meals I prepared were all food I enjoyed making, when I had the time. We sat down at the table. While we ate, I told her the reason I'd come.

"I want to tell you about five deaths. They're all cases in which people were murdered and their deaths were made to look accidental."

"Jesus, Gray," she said.

She got up and began making tea, though she'd only begun eating her meal. She didn't go on talking. I looked at her back.

"It's what I do," I said, not waiting for her to turn around. "You've been there with me. You know. And I need your help."

She faced me, leaning back against the counter, arms folded as if she was embracing herself. "What do you want me to do?"

"I need to know if a forensic pathologist can find signs that indicate murder, even very subtle signs, that an overworked medical examiner working on an accidental death theory might have missed."

"I could speculate about what's possible from a human-physiology point of view, if you tell me how they died. But I couldn't tell you anything for sure without going over the autopsy reports or looking at the bodies. And I'm no expert at that. Last time, we got lucky."

I nodded. "I understand. Just tell me what you can."

"How did they die?"

I started with the ones that had been to court already, the woman who'd been blown off the train platform, the carpenter who'd fallen off the building, and the man who'd been crushed. I told her about them one at a time.

"There's no difference," she said, shaking her head. "Being pushed off a platform, whether by the wind or by a person, isn't going to make a difference in the way a person dies. If someone knocked the woman unconscious, or beat her up, and then pushed her over the edge, that's different. But if all some- one did was push her off, there won't be any signs of that."

She said the same was true for the carpenter. And the man at the navy yard had been crushed so severely that no useful information could be detected by autopsy. We weren't getting anywhere. She was telling me, in effect, that someone had found a way to commit undetectable crimes. I told her about John Stein.

"That's the accident version, right?" she asked. "That he crashed his bike, fell, and was hit by the bus? What do you think really happened?"

"My guess is that the police version and the pathology report are accurate in every way but one: The bicycle accident never happened. It was staged. He was killed first and left with his bike on the road to be hit."

"It's no different," she said. "Any injury he suffered when they assaulted him could have happened either when he sup- posedly fell or as a result of being hit by the bus. And if they did a good job of staging it, they would have known what injuries to inflict to make it look like it was an accidental fall from the bike."

It bothered me more, somehow, that even John Stein's death, the one I could prove was a murder, was undetectable from a pathologist's point of view. I told her about the only other wrongful death case I had seen, the twenty-seven-year-old woman who died in the townhouse fire.

"If she was killed before the fire started, there's a way to tell," Molly said. "People who die in fires breathe in smoke and flame. Their lungs are smoke-scarred and burned. The only way that wouldn't happen is if the person was dead before the fire started, and therefore didn't breathe."

"I don't know if they killed her before they set the fire or if they only knocked her out. If she was unconscious, would it work the same?"

"No," Molly said. "Even unconscious, she'd be breathing at about the same rate and the smoke would damage her lungs."

There was no way the killer could know for sure that a drug or a blow meant to knock out the woman had not killed her. I'd go to the medical examiner's office to get a copy of a blank autopsy form. That part was easy. The ones with the names and details already filled in are kept confidential, but nobody kept watch over blank forms. I could forge the pathology report, as if the woman's body had been exhumed and examined again. It didn't matter that it was a forgery because I never intended to take it to court.

It would work. I had the Stein case witness and, on this one, a bluff he couldn't refute. I didn't need all five. I only had to convince Hartman I'd uncovered the pattern. It was time to deal.

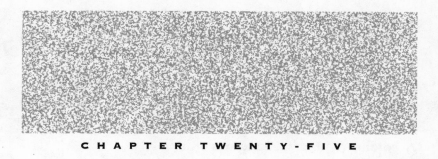

CHAPTER TWENTY-FIVE

I was ready by the evening but I waited until the next morning. Mornings were better—a lesson of the years. As the day went by, these guys got harder to reason with because their days rarely humbled them in any way. By the afternoons, they'd usually had so many pleasurable and self-important experiences, they got bloated with faith in their powers of persuasion and their immunity to ordinary rules. But in the mornings, if it was early enough on a routine day, they still had a little bit in them of the guy who looked in the mirror and saw time moving along.

Before entering his building, I wondered if I was putting myself at risk, if I would have to deal with any hired hands or traps. So far, he'd come at me twice, three times if I counted Dickson and the jail. But this was a visit directly for business and in his own place. I hoped that was enough to keep him out of his violent mode. To do anyone good, I had to survive. I walked up and pushed on the door.

The receptionist had a short skirt and long hair. I had an introduction ready but I didn't have to use it. As soon as I gave her my name I was in, no sitting and waiting required. He had told his receptionist I'd be showing up. I wondered in what other ways he was prepared.

The woman took me to his door. She knocked and opened

it for me when he answered, but she didn't go in. It was easy to tell that Hartman made the biggest bucks in the place. Offices are very clear badges. He didn't get up. His desk was unusual, a big slab of shiny black stone resting on two isolated wedges of steel, no drawers. Everything he used was out in the open on top of the slab—the phone, in and out files, and all the supplies. According to his desk, no secrets or lies.

I didn't have a good guess at his approach. He'd already displayed too wide a range. And we weren't starting from scratch. I wondered where he'd want to go.

"George Herman Gray. You played in the minor leagues. Were you named after the Babe?" He'd discovered something about me and wanted me to know.

I didn't bother telling him how I felt. It wasn't that the anger had gone away, but I was saving it for something else.

"I'm here to offer you a deal, which you'll make," I said. "Your part is, everybody you cheated gets paid."

"What do you mean?" He looked puzzled. It was indistinguishable from his genuine state of mind.

I took the insurance list out of my pocket and slid it across the desk. He took it, actually read it, and handed it back.

"I make a lot of money," he said. "So people come to me with deals all the time. That's your list. Here's mine." He held his hand up, palm out. He showed me the numbers as he went. "I've been threatened by you." One finger. "I've been hit by you." Another. "I've been followed." Another. Then he lifted a fourth finger, but he didn't point it at me. "I've been sued. I've been on trial." I hadn't sued him or put him on trial, but the hand stayed up. "And nothing's happened to me and no one's ever gotten what they came to me for. Maybe I'm not who they—or you—think I am."

"Everything you're talking about is business," I said. "But I'm talking about murder, and that's something else."

I laid out my facts about the killings.

"All those people who want you, they'll be able to get you now," I said. "I'm going to give them hope, get their spirits up again. And then the police are going to come in here and drag you out in handcuffs, which you know they really love to do. And the DA's going to make a nice name for himself with these hard-voting folks in the Northeast by putting you on trial."

I could see him shift to the state of mind he thought he needed. A second before, he was the weary giant, sniped at by the jealous weak. Suddenly that was gone. In its place was another kind of man.

"So you know about the murders," he said. "I may as well tell you, then. I figured that out too. It took me a long time. I'm usually smarter than that. But I don't traffic in violence the way you obviously think I do. Your big secret is that my own clients, who are also people I care about, were murdered? I already know it. They were chosen for killing. But not by me."

He was giving me a confession, but not his own.

"That's why I asked you to come see me. I noticed the pattern, I assume the same one you found. I did some investigating myself. I know who the killer is. It's someone I trusted, maybe someone you've trusted, too."

"If you have something to say, say it."

"Rachel Curren, of course. And I'm not just guessing, the way you are about me."

"You don't get out of this deal at all, Hartman, no matter what you say."

He sighed. "Look, you hate me, for whatever reason, so let's see if I can convince you. The only thing I've waited for is to have things solid enough to go to the police without taking the chance they'd think I took part. So you be the test. I know you've been with her, but maybe you didn't think you were with a killer. Do you have a taste for that?"

I didn't say anything, which he took as a sign to go on. Maybe it was.

"In a killing a few weeks ago there were witnesses who saw Rachel at the scene. I learned this only in the past few days. They didn't see her do anything, it's circumstantial, but it's still strong evidence. I know she did it because everything adds up. What do I get out of killing these people? She's the one who got the money. And then there's this."

He pulled a folder out from one of the neat piles of paper on the desk. He leaned across and handed it to me. I knew that he was the magician doing his act, that my reading his papers was the crucial audience participation needed for the trick to work. But I wanted to read it as much as he wanted me to. I opened the file.

I was holding copies of documents, parts of the writing hidden or excised; they were copies from faded, old paper. I was holding a social worker's notes from a foster agency record, according to the stamp. Hartman waited until I was halfway through the first page and then he started talking and never stopped, background narration for the pages in my hand. I hardly had to read. Hartman's voice droned out a summary, speaking the printed words aloud.

"If she did that when she was a child," he said, "then what's happened to my clients isn't such a stretch. She's the one who's violent. Not me.

"Look at the pattern. Heavy drinking after each of the murders. And then inpatient rehab to dry out. The first one in there's from Bucks County General. But after that, she had money from her first million-dollar case. So she went to a better place, Silver Springs. After that, she was rolling. See the next one, at Betty Ford. I checked. Twenty-five thousand dollars for her two weeks. And always after the murders. So what does that tell you?"

I looked at the second page from the Betty Ford Center.

"I got that from her roommate at the clinic," Hartman said. "It has a statement from Rachel, something she said in one of those exercises they make you do, where they tell you to be completely open and tell some secret truths."

The statement didn't say she murdered, but it talked about deaths and guilt. I had to agree with Hartman; it wasn't much of a stretch.

"I know I shouldn't even have some of this stuff," he said, now contrite. "I admit I used my money and connections to track this down. But I'm protecting myself, okay? And what I did in my investigation, even if I broke some rules—it's small stuff compared to murder. I have to defend myself, because it could easily look like I'm involved. You think I am. I referred those cases to her and those were my families!"

He would have been a great lawyer himself, I thought. He was good at making a plea.

"This all might not fit your opinion of me and your sexual interest in her. Can't blame you. That body, the looks, everything. But things didn't happen the way you think they did, like it or not."

"There's an eyewitness who saw you at one of the murders," I said.

I was looking at him closely, just in case, but there was nothing to see. He didn't react, and it was the best shot I had.

"And what does this eyewitness say?" he asked, in unworried calm.

"That a man carried John Stein's unconscious body and his bike down the block to the trolley line. You know, where the bus supposedly hit him while he was riding?"

I expected denial, but he had more than that.

"How do you know it was a man?"

I shook my head to suggest he was going in the wrong direction, but he went on.

"You know how strong she is. She's smart and big. Most women couldn't carry a guy and a bike, but Rachel—sure, she could. She's probably stronger than you and me."

The mage played out his magic well. Between the files he had shown me and the logic he offered, there was at least the possibility that he was right. He had more information than I did on the killings, enough to give the DA another plausible story of what had happened. He succeeded, at least temporarily, in doing something most little gods could not: He called my bluff, held off the deal. I had no choice but to walk out of his office empty-handed and tell him I'd be back. He didn't gloat, though he could have. We'd played a high-stakes game. And he'd won.

CHAPTER TWENTY-SIX

The best con artists leave you with empty pockets and a blurred mind. And there's something else. As the hours pass, and you think, and go on a long run through the streets of Chestnut Hill, and think some more, every inch of your body begins to tell you you've been conned. They seem so believable when they're moving their shells and controlling the game. But when it's over and you're alone, you realize that the only thing they sold you was a bottle of sand. Everything Hartman said and showed me existed in his office only. It could have been as fabricated and phony as the medical records he'd shown Jerry. I hadn't even thought to ask him for copies.

What I needed to learn was whether Rachel was in the clear. I needed to examine things more genuine than a Hartman document. Until I knew that Rachel was innocent, I couldn't make a deal with Hartman.

Hartman's information suggested that Rachel lived a continuous path of violence from childhood on. If that was a lie, the rest of Hartman's story was likely to be false as well. Childhood records were difficult to get. But I had an easier way to look into the past. She had told me the place to go and it wasn't far away.

The phone book for Upper Bucks County had only one listing for a Curren; his name was Robert. That afternoon I drove the forty-five miles to Springtown, straight north on

309, past the endless malls and newly built townhouse blocks. I cut off onto smaller roads, where a scenic, rural edge held out against the developers. That part of Springtown was small and still looked old.

The thick, wooden front door to the Curren house was open. I knocked anyway. It took a minute for someone to answer. The man who eventually came was about seventy-five. He had a full head of hair, and it was bone-white, pale and thin enough to see through. He was big, but the way he stood and moved was frail.

"Mr. Curren?"

He nodded.

"Who's there, Bob?"

I heard a woman's voice from inside the house.

"Are you related to Rachel Curren?" I asked.

The old man's eyes widened. He was leaning heavily on the door but some energy came to him for a second and he took a deep breath. A woman his age came out of the back of the house. She was wearing an apron and had a kitchen towel in her hands. Suppertime in Bucks County was fast approaching. Four o'clock and everything's all right. Except that I was there.

"What is it?" the woman asked.

"I'm Gray, a friend of Rachel's." I said it to both of them.

"I'm her uncle. We haven't heard a word from Rachel in fifteen years," the old man said.

"What do you want, Mr. Gray?" the woman said. It wasn't a challenge.

"I've gotten to know your niece," I said. "She's in some trouble and I want to help. But to do so, I need to know about her family and she won't tell me much."

The old man's expression didn't change. "Seems to me you ought to be asking her questions, not us."

He shifted his weight to close the door.

"I can help her," I said.

"Why don't you come in, young man," the old woman said.

I tried to follow her in but the old man didn't clear a path. Mrs. Curren turned around, noticed the barrier, and removed it with a word.

"Bob," she said in an easy voice.

The old man stepped aside. I walked into the house, following the old woman into a big square living room right off the front door. There was a musty smell that didn't come from a lack of cleanliness but from the passage of time. The furnishings and decorations hadn't changed in many years. This was a room that spoke of solidity and longevity. It took human activity and embraced it in muted tones of dark wood, furnishings of great weight, and deep cushions.

Mrs. Curren sat on one end of a large couch. There were also armchairs, deep and comfortable. Mr. Curren took one of those. I sat down on the other end of the couch.

I took a closer look around the room, as if it held the answers. The mantel over the fire pit held ten or fifteen gold-colored little oval photo stands. They were all informal shots of family members and friends. If Rachel was up there, perhaps the key to her mysteries was there as well.

"Which one of those is Rachel's parents?" I asked, pointing to the pictures.

"None of them are," the old man said, as if I should have known.

"Tell me about Rachel," I said. "Please."

"Rachel was an abused child, I'll tell you straight out," Mr. Curren said. "That's all you need to know."

Mrs. Curren nodded. "We didn't know what to do. She never talked about it, never said a thing. Back then, people didn't talk about these things."

"And it was over, that was the main thing," Mr. Curren said. "It was over and done with. We took her in, raised her the best we could. It didn't help her, or at least not enough."

"Tell him, Bob," the woman said. "Tell him what he wants to know."

"He'll blame us, believe me." He gestured toward me.

As both of them spoke, despite the sad story they told, I had the refreshing sense of being with decent, honest people. The contrast to Hartman was palpable. That feeling alone almost convinced me that Rachel was innocent, and that Hartman had schemed everything—the killings and the false accusations against Rachel.

"We knew something was wrong, even when she was very young," the woman said. "She'd say sometimes when she visited us that she didn't want to go home. She never said why. Then sometimes we'd see she was bruised. We talked to her mother about it once."

"Her mother?"

"Yes," Mrs. Curren said. "It was her mother who beat her, you know."

"And when we spoke to her," Mr. Curren said, "my sister got angry and didn't say a thing. She stormed out. But one night she was here and almost passed out drunk. And she talked about Rachel—so vile, the things she said.

"But we didn't do anything, which is maybe what Rachel blames us for. And not much after that, they died. We knew

Rachel never got over it, not in all the time we had her. And I guess what you're telling us is, not even to this day."

"How did they die? And when?"

"In a car accident," Mr. Curren said. "On Stone's Ferry Road, a few blocks out of town. It's a steep hill and a sharp curve. Comes up on you fast. The car went through the brush and into the trees, head on. All three were dead when the police got there. Lost the family all at once. She'd just had her tenth birthday and we had a big party for her here. She seemed happy, and then the next day, like that, they were gone."

"Three of them?"

"Her mother and father and her little brother, Danny. She was the only one left."

"I'm sorry," I said. "I had to know." I thanked them and let myself out.

The information they provided was consistent with what Hartman had suggested. Rachel had the potential to be very dangerous. Hartman had done his homework well. But she had been raised by these loving people and not in a foster home. If Hartman had fabricated those papers, then he had serious intentions to bury Rachel along with his deeds. My appearance had to have sped up the process. I headed back to Chestnut Hill. I called Rachel on the way.

CHAPTER TWENTY-SEVEN

We had left it open as to where we'd meet. I expected to call her again once I got home but she was waiting for me when I arrived. She seemed to like Chestnut Hill.

"Didn't think I'd get here before you," she said. "A major traffic jam on Seminole. Three cars. One of them tried to park."

"This isn't social. We have some decisions to make."

"So let's talk," she said. "But can we also walk?"

We walked toward Seminole down Rex. Her pace was fast. We were silent for a block.

"I went up to Springtown. I met your aunt and uncle."

"You talked to my aunt and uncle." She repeated it as if she didn't understand what I said.

"Yes," I said. "And they told me a lot. It helped me make sense of what happened in my house the other night. But that wasn't why I went there. It was to finish looking into the problem I originally came to see you about."

"So tell me what you think you know," she said.

I didn't hesitate; uncovering things and telling people about them was what I did. It was what the victims were owed.

"There is insurance fraud, I can prove it. The person responsible for the insurance scam is Jim Hartman. There's more than insurance fraud—and I've connected two people to all of it, two people you know. One is Hartman. The other is Ronald Dickson, the judge."

"Tell me what they've done," she said, as if she took it for granted that they were criminals and all Rachel lacked in understanding was the details. She turned away from me so I couldn't see her face. I didn't know what she was thinking or feeling.

"I've found twenty-four cases so far in which Hartman sold life insurance policies, a family member died, and no death benefit was paid. He's collecting the premiums, not passing along the money to the company, and keeping it himself. When someone dies, he makes up an excuse that seems plausible to the family and he settles with them for a small amount. That's a fraud worth millions by itself. But I came across something worse."

She didn't say anything this time. I wondered if what I'd told her so far was any kind of a surprise, and even if it wasn't, if she knew what was coming next. I didn't like talking to her back. I wanted to see the effect of what I was saying. I moved up to her and grabbed her arm, lightly, to turn her my way. She didn't pull away and she didn't turn around. I stepped in front of her so she could see me. Her eyes were closed. She seemed frozen in place. She looked stiff and frightened, like a child bracing for a blow. She had good reason.

"I've found five cases in which people died in what appeared to be accidents and in which wrongful-death lawsuits were filed. The people who died were all in their mid-twenties, middle-class, with big lifetime earning potential. You know even better than I do that those are the characteristics of big-money wrongful-death suits, millions of dollars guaranteed. You were the lawyer in all five cases. All five of those families were carrying life insurance policies sold by Hartman."

She opened her eyes and looked at me. She was trembling, but she still didn't speak.

"I've already told you that John Stein is one of those cases," I said, sounding as grim as I felt. "I'm convinced he, and the other four, were murdered. I have evidence."

She looked at me and I couldn't read her expression. "Nightmares coming true," she said. She spoke softly enough to be talking to herself. It wasn't denial or admission. It was as if she herself wasn't sure what she did or didn't know. She stooped over slowly. She put her hands to her head, covering her face. I went on.

"Hartman is in business with Judge Dickson. And you were Dickson's law clerk five years ago. There's been a conspiracy to commit those murders, to make them look like accidents, to have them represented in court by you, to have you win. You, Hartman, and Dickson are linked in so many ways. I know Hartman referred the victims' families to you. I know Dickson is dirty. I know Hartman's a thief. I'm hoping you weren't knowingly involved. It's possible you were used. Everyone—the police, the insurance companies' investigators, a jury in three cases so far—believed the deaths were accidental. Maybe you did, too. But you made a lot of money from those cases, millions of dollars in the past few years. You were the lawyer who made the scheme work. Maybe you even helped kill people. Tell me."

"I knew. I should have known. I knew the judge was rotten when I was his clerk. And I didn't do anything about it. I let him do what he wanted. I was blind to Jim. It's all my fault."

She wasn't making enough sense for me to follow. I had to have things clear. I reached for her and pulled her to her feet. She didn't resist.

"You're going to tell me everything right now. If you're guilty, it's all coming out and you're going to jail. The best thing you can do for yourself, and the only chance you have, is to tell me everything. If you tell me the truth, I'll do what I can to help you. If you're innocent—and I hope you are—then now's the time to tell me. Because I can keep you out of the way of what happens. I want to do that because I like you, because I know something about you, and because if you're innocent, that's what really matters, and you shouldn't be hurt."

"I'm not innocent," she said. "The cases were too perfect to be real. And Jim kept coming up with them, didn't he? I was so blind." The sound she made was too raw to be a laugh or a cry. "I killed everyone, and they're gone, and it's been twenty years, and whatever it is about me, it started with killing."

She wasn't even looking at me. She was talking to herself. I braced myself for a confession I needed to hear. If she had had a hand in creating victims, then there really wasn't anything I could do to help her. But she could do something for me, give me more of what I needed to take the others down.

"I'm a killer, yes. I killed my own family. But I didn't kill John Stein, or any of the others I represented. I didn't know about that. I even called Jim after I first met you to tell him you were investigating. I didn't think he'd done anything wrong. I'm blind and I'm a fool. And I poison everything I touch. That's what I do. I thought I was helping families, helping people. I thought despite everything, I had grown up to be able to help other people, even if I couldn't help myself."

She fell silent. It looked as if she wanted to say more, but whatever she was feeling choked her up and she couldn't get the words out. I didn't know what to say. I believed she was innocent, was convinced of it more than if she had offered me an elaborate denial. She hadn't been part of the murders or the fraud, but she was standing there declaring her own guilt with more venom than any prosecutor would. I had been to the place it all started, talked to people who knew. I understood how her family had died and why she might have thought it was her fault. She hadn't killed her family, but she clearly felt guilty for their deaths. I didn't know how someone lived with that feeling.

We were walking on the long road to the McCallum Street Bridge. There were a few houses on one side of the road, but the other side was lined with pines and maples along a pasture that ran all the way to Fairmount Park. The greenery was offset by a long fieldstone wall. I stopped and leaned. She moved in a slow circle in front of me. I waited for her to say more. But she remained strangely silent.

We moved on to the bridge. The night had been still until that moment. I heard the sound of a distant car moving fast, coming our way at a good clip. The bridge was narrow. I edged us closer to the rail, looked over at the hundred-foot drop to low woods and a slim stream. The rush of tires and roar of an engine grew as the car gained speed. Both of us turned to look back at the road. The car was a block away, half off the road and on our path.

Rachel pointed to the far end of the bridge. "Come on, the other side."

She started running in an outright sprint. I followed. We were full speed, mouths open, turning seconds into great chunks of ground. I shot a glance back. There was no way to make it. My work used to be predicting the speed and distance of objects coming at me. I knew the car would hit us before we reached the other side.

I grabbed her shoulder. We needed to stop. There wasn't breath or time to explain.

"No good!" I yelled.

"What then?" she said.

The car swung onto the bridge. The driver was taking a chance at that speed. The few inches the sidewalks were raised off the asphalt and the low metal fence wouldn't have been enough to stop the car if it swerved for the edge. It would kill us but go over the side as well.

"One chance," I said. "Over the side."

I grabbed the short rail fence and so did she. The metal rust scraped my skin. It barely held our weight. We leaned out over air and hard ground a hundred feet below. The car was on the sidewalk twenty feet away.

I held on to the rail and swung over the low fence. I dropped down to the siding and let go. I got the firmest grip I could on the flat concrete. Rachel followed, right there at my side. The faded blue side of the car scraped the fence above us, which erupted in a shower of yellow and orange sparks. The whining shriek got louder, the car's advance a moving metal wall. I lowered my head and held my breath.

A piece of the rail ripped free, trailing sparks, straight at her face. She took one hand off the edge to protect herself, leaving her hanging on with the other. I let go with my left hand and grabbed her at the waist. I pulled her toward me and the two of us hung on, one hand each. The noise and metal fire peaked, then ebbed. We reached up in unison and got grips with our other hands.

Brakes screeched. My fingers were almost numb, slippery with blood and sweat. The strength she had in a lighter body gave her the ability to move. She was pulling herself hand over hand along the ledge toward a fencepost she could use to hoist herself up. A car door opened. I looked up. Hartman got out. He was always the man with a plan. I wondered what else he'd do.

He stopped and got back into the car. A second later, he put the car in reverse, picking up speed, coming toward us again. We both saw it. She had a chance. I couldn't get out of the way. Moments before he reached us, she made it to the post.

"Hold tight," I yelled.

I swung myself as far as I could to the right, barely holding on, then swung back to the left with all the momentum I could gather. Then I let go. I reached out and up and managed to grab her at the waist. She cried out when I hit, but held on. I pulled myself up on her body until I had the post.

The car hit the fence exactly where I'd been. The curve was too wide or the brakes couldn't stop it. The back wheels spat gravel and pieces of metal over the edge, then had more air than road. The front of the car rose straight up, then fell back fast as it cleared the bridge. Its underside faced us, the rest of it invisible, all through the long, hard drop to the trees. The crash was one continuous sound, finally louder when it hit the ground. Black dust, smoke of a fire, swirling wind rose up higher than the trees.

She pulled herself up while I held on. She leaned over and extended her hand. Taking it meant letting go of my grip. I did and she pulled me up to the ground. I stayed kneeling for a minute, leaning on the fence. She had both her hands on her head as if to protect herself from something falling from above.

I looked around. I didn't hear sirens but we probably had

very little time; the car crash had been loud. There weren't close neighbors to the bridge but someone was likely to call it in. When they arrived, I didn't want to be around. There still wasn't anything I wanted or needed from the police.

I looked over the edge. The smoke hadn't cleared. I thought I could see the car. It hadn't been Hartman's Cadillac but something older, big, and steel. We would have had no chance if he had hit us, at whatever speed. He was good at setups, I thought. A stolen car, a drunk driver run off, Rachel and I dead, on or under the bridge. But Hartman had the accident this time, and he was below, dead and gone. Now I heard sirens in the distance. I turned back to Rachel. She was also gone.

CHAPTER TWENTY-EIGHT

Twenty-four hours passed. I had been to Rachel's home and office twice and called there a dozen times. She was off in the void and I wasn't sure what that meant. I had to consider going after her. For one thing, I didn't know what, if anything, she knew about the murders. For another, she had the only money I could tap, now that Hartman was gone. But in the end I didn't have to go after her. Again, she came to me. She knocked on my door late at night.

"I had to leave last night," she said. "I drove around, walked around. I drove to Springtown, my parents' old place, then to my aunt's house. I haven't been there in a long time. They knew something was wrong, but I didn't tell them what. When this is over, if I can, I'll go back."

We were in my living room. She took a deep breath. She was businesslike, making a report.

"I've kept things back from you, but nothing involving crimes. At least, I had no idea there were crimes. I knew Hartman well. I slept with him for a while, five years ago. That stopped, but the business didn't. He referred cases to me I never would have gotten on my own, incredible cases of wrongful deaths. I liked presenting them and they were hard to lose. In return for the cases, I gave him forty percent of the contingency fees I received. That may seem illegal, but it's not. It's commonly done, though usually the finder's fee for the referral is much less. I didn't know about the killings. I can't stand knowing about them now."

"And the judge?"

"He was how Hartman got to me. When I clerked for Dickson, I saw Hartman come to his office routinely. They were close friends."

"Not just friends. I told you, they did business together, too."

A quizzical look. She didn't know that part of it, so I told her.

"Dickson was Hartman's personal insurance. Fraud that made it to court got settled or got thrown out. Dickson made sure."

She nodded. "You said he had me set up."

"He did a great job of it, too. He showed me files, phonied up a lot, I assume. He was impressed with your drinking. So was I, in fact. But he had you at a rehab center in Montgomery County. He also had you at the Betty Ford Center. He had you doing the cure after each of the killings, proof of your involvement and remorse. DAs love that kind of stuff. Truth?"

"Yes to drinking a lot, of course. You've seen that close up. But I haven't had any problems like that. Maybe I've just been lucky, or I haven't had the bad luck yet. But no, no rehab."

"He had convincing stuff, documents. Lots of them. There's probably even more convincing stuff in his files. But I suspect it was his hedge if the murders turned up. If I can help it, they won't. So you might not have to worry."

"I'm worried anyway," she said. "I worried enough to leave last night. What ended up happening?"

"You didn't see the papers?" I had three different editions on the table. I handed her one. The *Chestnut Hill Local* did the best job this time. The cover was a photo of the bridge and the wreckage. The photo below the crease was a smaller shot of the broken rail and the trees, looking down, a reminder of the distance to the ground. The path the car had taken was marked by broken branches, the damage invisible to me last night. The story was that a drunken driver in a stolen car had crashed and they hadn't yet identified the man.

She ended up looking at all three papers. "You're not going to tell them?"

"To what end? He tried to kill us. He's still going to pay for that. If I go to the police, or if you do, it all unravels. I don't want the murders uncovered, or anything publicized either. I still have work to do."

"Tell me what," she said. "I want to help."

"Tell me something first," I said. "You were so wrapped up with this guy for years in different ways. How did you manage not to know what he was like?"

She waited awhile and so did I. But once she started talking it was a long time before she stopped.

"I'm an expert at not knowing when people are screwing me around, or why," she said. "My mother hit me. I never knew why. She'd have some kind of fit, throw me on the floor, pull my hair, bang my head on the wall. She beat me with whatever she could grab—a wooden spoon, I remember that. I had bruises. I was always afraid people would see. When they did, though, nothing changed.

"She used to get upset about my looks. People told me I was pretty, said it in front of her all the time. It bothered her, I knew that. When I was six, she decided I was too impressed with myself. That was the way she put it.

"She used to knit. I was always afraid of the needles. But the worst thing she did was use them the way they were meant to be used. She knitted a thing—it started out as a hat. She made a face for it, like a mask but without any holes. When she made me wear it I could hardly breathe. If I took it off, she'd beat me, or threaten to. She took it off before my father got home. So it was good when he was home, at first.

"My father and my mother didn't talk much. She'd mostly get out of his way. He'd come into my room to talk. I knew he saw the bruises if she'd beaten me that day. He'd tell me I was pretty. He'd turn off the lights and close the door. He told me touching him would make me feel better. When I was with him, sometimes I wished I had the mask.

"By nine, my father had been coming to me for almost five years. He mentioned my tenth birthday coming up a lot. I was getting too old for our games. He said once he was worried I'd get pregnant. We kept going, but he started promising me things for my birthday.

"When I turned ten, he said, he'd stop coming to my room. I'd be too old then. He called it my 'graduation day.' Weeks before my birthday I was counting the days. I believed it but I doubted it too. So I got him to promise me something—a lock for my room. It only meant changing the doorknob to one you could lock from inside. After he agreed, I was especially nice to him the days before it came. I let him do things he always wanted to do. I pretended it didn't hurt me because I was older now.

"On my birthday we had a party at my aunt and uncle's house. It was nice, despite everything. I had a talent for keeping the bad stuff apart. I was excited when we got home. I checked to see if he had kept his promise. And there it was. It was the best I had felt in a long time.

"That night I stayed in my room with the door locked. Until

then I never felt the room was really mine. I had special secret things hidden away, little dumb things, plastic dolls and animals, an odd-shaped stick I found in the woods, a picture I'd been given by a boy in my class. I took them all out. I put them on top of the dresser in plain sight. They were mine. It was my room. I lay there and every few minutes I opened my eyes to see all my things. I felt good, really good.

"In the middle of the night I heard a noise outside my door. I looked over at the new doorknob and I saw it start to turn. I didn't make a sound. I remember I closed my eyes. The knob turned, the door opened. I knew he was there. I opened my eyes. He had the damn key in his hand. He came to my bed, like all the other nights. He was drunk. He said, 'Sorry, baby, but I need you. I can't help myself.'

"The next morning my mother yelled at me and hit me, even in front of him. She asked me how I liked sleeping with the lock on the door, now that I was big. I wouldn't talk to her or to my father either. I didn't care anymore.

"That afternoon they went out to do some errands in town. They took my little brother with them, left me alone in the house. I sat there, watched it get dark outside. I got up, put on my jacket, and went out. The road to town is Stone's Ferry. There's a bridge near my house across Ferry Creek. It's a steep hill, there's a curve at the bottom with a drop-off to the woods on one side when it flattens out. Cars come fast across the bridge. The curve is sharp enough they can't see much ahead.

"I decided I'd get it all over, go out there and get hit by a car. I went to the bottom of the hill, by the curve. It was completely dark. I stood in the middle of the road on the bridge. I waited for a car to come.

"I closed my eyes but I could still see the brightness of headlights coming up. I was glad. I didn't move at all. I knew the car couldn't stop. The brakes made a sound like screaming.

"I heard screaming for real, familiar voices, and I opened my eyes. It was only for a second, but I could see. My father was driving and he saw me. My mother was hanging on to his arm. My brother was in the back seat.

"The car went right to avoid me, off the road, off the bridge into the trees. I heard the glass smash to bits, then silence when it hit the water. I didn't even stay to see. I walked home. It was like I never left the house. I put my jacket back on the peg. I didn't know what else I did until someone came to the door. It was my aunt and the police."

"I didn't die then, I don't die now. I've been living since then. Some kind of life." Her voice trailed off. Now she sounded tired. "I slept with the judge too," she said. She grimaced. "My choice." She shook her head. "I've been used by so many people. How was I supposed to know what Hartman or Dickson was really like? To me, they were just two more people who used me. That's a pretty weak excuse, I know. But it's the truth."

It hardly seemed weak to me. In fact, she answered all the questions I could imagine asking.

"Tell me what you're going to do," she said. "I want to help."

C H A P T E R   T W E N T Y · N I N E

Dickson's courtroom was in an office building, but his chambers were on the sixth floor of Philadelphia's City Hall. His court session would be ending shortly. I waited on an uncomfortable bench down the corridor and watched the elevator. She waited by the door. She had called for an appointment. As far as Dickson knew, Rachel was his only visitor.

I looked down the corridor at the line of green doors. Each one led to a courtroom. People entered those rooms with hope, but it wasn't their place. Courtrooms belonged to Dickson and the other judges. He had given me a little reminder of his power. It was power I could use.

Shortly after four, he got out of the elevator and headed for the door marked RONALD DICKSON, COMMON PLEAS COURT JUDGE. He greeted Rachel with a hand on her arm as if she were long lost and welcome, and with no hint that his business partner had tried to kill her two nights earlier. You had to be very good with lies to act that smoothly.

I couldn't hear any of what he said to her. They went in. I waited a few minutes, then followed. I wasn't absolutely sure Dickson knew what Hartman had done. Either way, he wasn't going to be glad to see me. I didn't know how close he'd let me get or how long he'd want me to stay. But it wasn't his choice.

He had locked the door behind them, but Rachel unlocked

it. I let myself in. His private office was a contrast to the rest of City Hall. City Hall was dirty but his chambers were another world, of oriental rugs, hand-carved cabinets, and wood walls. He was already comfortable, in a big leather chair behind a big desk. He hadn't yet taken off his robes. If he was feeling uneasy about seeing me, he didn't let it show.

He looked at Rachel. When she said nothing, he turned to me.

"Mr. Gray. What's this all about?"

"Business. You know that. I've got some evidence you need to hear about. Then we talk. You can try to convince me not to take it to the U.S. Attorney."

"I'm a judge," he said. "I'm the one around here who talks to U.S. attorneys and sends people to jail, not you."

He raised his voice. He got a little red. I felt good about that. What I was holding to force a deal with Dickson was stronger than my usual hook. As a lawyer, Rachel understood immediately what worked best.

"Tell him." I looked to Rachel. And she did.

It was as if she were testifying in front of a jury. She described each murder in detail, leaving out nothing—but adding something. She said that she and Dickson had participated in all the planning, and often helped in the actual killings. What she said about her role and the judge's were lies, but that didn't matter. She was willing to give up her life to make it work. She was prepared to confess—to the authorities, if needed—to seven homicides. By that one stroke she made herself an ironclad eyewitness to the deaths, providing firsthand evidence that Hartman and the judge were guilty. If Dickson forced her to go public, it would mean she had surrendered her place in the world. But the potential sacrifice would only increase her credibility. The threat of her testimony was going to be strong enough to bring the judge down.

She was clever. She described each "accident" from a killer's point of view. There were the five I saw in the court records and two that hadn't yet become a lawsuit, two women who were killed in the past month. Rachel was the only person other than Hartman who could convincingly describe the deaths. She knew every detail, because a lawyer required a killer's familiarity with how victims died.

I didn't make her finish. I took out a deposition she had already prepared before we got to the judge's chamber. It contained a complete summary of murder and fraud by the three of them. I slid the deposition over to Dickson.

"She has a lot to say. This sums it up. Why don't you look?"

He took ten minutes to read it through. Then he stood up.

"You're crazy!" He yelled it at her.

She didn't say anything back. I needed her silent. We had to make him deal with me.

"She's lying," he said. He stared at me as if expecting agreement.

I shook my head. "Not likely she'd lie about something so serious," I said. "Why would she confess to multiple murders she didn't commit? That's what most people will think."

"Her statement is worthless. A total fabrication."

"I agree with you. I think she's lying too—about her role in the murders. But everything else she said is true, isn't it? You'll go down on conspiracy for the murders. You first took Hartman's money when you agreed to fix a case against him nine years ago. And more since then. And Hartman conveniently created his own files that implicate Rachel in the killings. So she's got Hartman's evidence to back up her story. That's a hell of a lot of credibility, wouldn't you say?"

"She's a very unstable woman trying to beat a murder rap. It won't get to me."

"Maybe her testimony won't stand alone. But the DA will look at each of the murders. He knows there are insurance companies out there interested in the possibility they were bilked out of millions of dollars. The city lost big money too. They'll find trails from Hartman to Rachel to you, the same way I did. They'll make a case independent of her testimony. Combine Rachel on the witness stand and the paper trail of fraud, and you don't stand a chance in front of a jury. So long to your black robe, your willing clerks, your fancy chambers, and all the other things that go with being a judge. And all because you wouldn't deal with me. Now isn't that stupid?"

"Why don't you tell me what the hell you want."

"As far as I know there are twenty-four families who had phony Hartman life insurance policies when one of the family members died. By rough calculations he owes five point six million in death benefits to those families. You're going to see that the families are paid every dime."

"What are you talking about?" the judge said. "I had nothing to do with Hartman's life insurance business. Why talk to me about his problems?"

"They're your problems now. That's part of our deal. You covered him, profited with him, and you're the one who's left. I don't care how you get the money. I'd prefer if it came from Hartman's estate. You can do it. This is Philadelphia. We both know how probate court works. You get in there first thing in the morning and get yourself made executor of his estate. Pull whatever strings you have to pull. That gives you access to all his accounts and leaves it up to you to distribute his money. I'll show you where the money goes. You just handle the paper-work and make sure the checks go out. After that, you get to live in this chamber as long as you like. Nobody gets Rachel's statement. Everything I know remains secret. And once you pay off the people on that list, you never see me—or either of us—again."

I pulled an envelope out of my jacket and tossed it on his desk. In it were the names and addresses and dollar amounts owed to the twenty-four families. Jerry's name was first. I'd doubled the death benefit for him. My own name was in there too. I'd been meaning to get some life insurance.

"And there's John Stein, Mary Cooper, and Tracy Lucas. Their families won't get to civil court now that Rachel's dropped out. I want you to discover that all three of them were covered by some special policy Hartman had written for them that their families obviously didn't know about. You pay them a death benefit of a million dollars each. You can take all the money from Hartman's estate. But if he doesn't have enough, then you pay."

He didn't say anything and he didn't look at either of us. Instead, he looked at a side door to his office. The door opened.

"Good plan. Don't you think it works better if I'm dead?" It was Hartman. He was calm, as if he'd been sitting in the room with us all along.

"Oh God," Rachel said. I didn't say anything, but I had the same reaction. Then I wondered how Hartman had managed the disappearing trick at the bridge, until I realized it was hardly a big deal for such a polished magician. There literally was smoke and fire at the scene. But who was the unidentified body a hundred feet below the bridge? I'd probably never find out.

"We have no problems," Hartman said, turning to Rachel. "If you want to confess to the murders, that's fine. I already told Gray you were guilty." He smiled at her. "Have an attack of conscience, babe?"

"I should have had one a long time ago," she said.

"Well, this is great," Dickson said to Hartman. "It's a big damn mess."

"It is," I said, "only if you try to protect Hartman."

"Shut up," Hartman said. He turned to the judge. "Let them leave," he said. "Just let them. It's dangerous out there. They already know that." He smiled at us. "They won't last long."

I ignored him. It was the only trick I had. I talked to the judge.

"Hartman can't avoid prosecution and conviction," I said. "He's done too much and it's been uncovered. House of cards. My lawyer's got Rachel's deposition and one of my own. Sam Hatton at Deckert Price. Go ahead, give him a call. He's expecting it. Protect Hartman and you go down with him. It makes no difference whether Rachel and I are killed. Both of you take the fall if we die."

Dickson looked at his telephone. He decided to test my story. He pulled out a legal directory and called Sam. He talked to him for only a few seconds, then hung up.

Hartman stood up, then leaned his hands on Dickson's desk. "Why are you playing this game?" Hartman yelled, and for the first time he sounded annoyed.

I talked faster, and only to the judge.

"One right word and all this gets unraveled. You know it. All of Hartman's schemes depend on guts and charm, on no one getting to the bottom of his pit. But it's all come undone. There's nothing left, no one to con and no way to do it. The truth is clear: He's crazy. Are you crazy too?"

"Call your guards and have them taken out," Hartman said.

"I have to think!" the judge said.

"About what?" Hartman yelled. "Why are you even listening to him?"

Hartman turned to leave. The judge stood up and undid his robe. He was holding a gun. I wasn't surprised by that. In Philadelphia, that was part of a judge's outfit, as common as a pen. But he was pointing it at me.

"Now you're thinking," Hartman said. "The two of them busted in on us having a meeting and threatened you. You have no choice. You have to shoot them. Self-defense. It works."

"I can get away with it," the judge said, still talking to me. "You're a freelance something with a shady past. I had you locked up for contempt and you spent a night in jail. You got angry. You got into my chambers and tried to kill me. I protected myself. I could shoot you both and have time to figure something out. I have the room so soundproofed I could shoot off a cannon in here without it being heard. The benefit of doing lots of private deals."

If not for the gun I would have felt that I was where I wanted to be. I convinced myself I was and went ahead.

"Think about it, Dickson. You're used to making decisions. Make a good one. You want to add two more murders to the charges against you? Or do you want to get out of this whole mess and go on with your life? Do this Hartman's way and you have nothing in front of you but murder charges and jail time, at best. And for one dumb reason: because you shot us instead of thinking clearly."

He didn't put the gun down, but he didn't shoot it either. Hartman's patience ran out.

"Give me the fucking gun."

Hartman stepped toward the desk. The judge waved him off.

"Shut up," the judge said. "Just stand there for a minute."

"What? No time for that now. Give me the gun!"

The judge stepped back and leveled the gun at Hartman. Hartman rushed toward the desk and lunged for the judge.

"Stop it!" Dickson shouted. "Calm down!"

"Give me the fucking gun, you idiot," Hartman yelled. Then he reached for it. The judge fired. Hartman fell. Rachel moved toward him, caught him before he went down. I reached across the desk and took the gun away. Rachel let Hartman's body drop.

"He's dead," she said.

I bent down to check his neck. When I stood up, the judge was sitting down.

"Let's finish our business," he said.

I was too stunned to speak.

"Now his estate's available," Dickson said. "But let's go over it one more time. I pay everyone on your list and you just go away? Nothing goes to the police, the DA, or the U.S. Attorney? That's it?"

"Hartman did the killing. Hartman's dead. The people he hurt get paid. You're going to see to it. I'm not interested in any more justice than that. You can do the victims more good as a judge than as an inmate." I looked at Rachel. So did the judge.

"Justice enough," she said.

"Okay, it's a deal," the judge said. "Get out of the building and then I'll call the police. Hartman attacked me because he thought I was going to have him arrested for insurance fraud. He tried to kill me, and I shot him in self-defense."

I looked at the judge, but before I could say anything he did.

"Of course, because I shot Hartman, it wouldn't make sense for me to execute his will. Don't worry about it. I already know exactly who will do it. He'll do everything I say, guaranteed. He's a hundred percent reliable. There'll be no problems—Hartman doesn't even have any heirs. Because of the shooting, it will take several weeks to get the checks out. But it's a done deal."

I had no doubt the judge wanted to finish the deal as soon as possible. He saw how close he had come to losing everything. Before leaving, I took the gun and wiped it clean so the cops wouldn't find my prints. Then I picked up the deposition from Dickson's desk and tucked it away. Rachel opened the door and I followed her out.

CHAPTER THIRTY

I drove through Fairmount Park to Roxborough, taking the same route Jerry and I had walked a few weeks earlier. By night, the park road was silent and black. I parked a few blocks from Jerry's house and saw a small crowd piling out of a shopping center movie theater, loud and laughing.

I walked slowly to Jerry's, clearing my head. Things in the judge's chamber had gone well, but they never go well enough. Hartman was dead and Dickson was in his cage, following my orders. That was good. As far as Hartman went, I knew the judge had done me a favor. Hartman had turned out to be a killer, not only a little god of schemes. He needed to be put away, any way he could. I always counted on a law of nature to set things right, a theory I had that killers usually met up with their own kind, criminals or cops, and, like warring armies, whittled their own numbers down. On average, the theory worked, but not in every case. This time, it had worked out exactly that way.

The good part was that the victims I'd been able to identify were going to get the money they were due. The bad part was that money was the only solution I ever had. The world didn't offer endless choices. If I hadn't had the judge, I would have needed Hartman alive to make my deal. With Hartman gone, I needed the judge. Dickson deserved to be in jail, at least. But

Dickson jailed or Dickson dead would put the victims' money out of reach. I wondered if I'd ever get one of these cases completely right.

I had called Jerry to say I'd be by at midnight. I figured even Sean would be sleeping by then. Jerry came to the door. I could tell from the silence of the house behind him that I had come late enough; the baby was also asleep.

"It's done," I said. "Your money's on the way."

He grinned, shook his head. "How did you—"

"That's the good part of what I do—it works. Though sometimes it gets a little"—I thought about Rachel, and everything else—"complicated."

"You mean Hartman?"

I told him about Byberry. "Did Sean tell you?"

"I can't believe he kept it to himself," he said. "No, he didn't tell me."

"I'm not surprised. He was sure you'd go after Hartman."

"So how come you're telling me now?"

I told him about the bridge.

"That was Hartman! But the papers—" He thought about it. "And the police." He thought some more. "You're not going to tell them, are you?"

"Blackmail doesn't work without secrets."

I still hadn't made up my mind how to raise the issue of Sean. I couldn't imagine Karen lying to Jerry, even by omission. He knew Sean wasn't his. He knew Karen was with me right before she met him. He had to have known Sean was mine, all these years. But no one had ever said a word, at least not to me. I wondered what it would mean, or lead to, to say these things aloud.

"There's something else about Sean," I blurted out.

Jerry had stood up to get us coffee. He took a step back. He looked upstairs.

"He's okay," I said. "It's not that. It's about Karen. And me."

Jerry waited for me to say more.

"Tell me about Sean," I said. "Jerry, I have to know."

"Look, Gray, please. I don't know what to tell you."

"The truth, that's all. I looked up the birth certificate. The dates are right for me and wrong for you. Trust me, Jerry. You know I'm not going to do anything. But I have to know. It's not something I can walk away from without knowing the truth. You can understand."

"If you know it, why are you asking me?"

"I don't know it. I think it. It's the way I do my business. I get partway by looking things up in records, and then I take the world's best guesses. In this case that's not good enough. I need to know. She's gone. I can't ask her. Tell me, Jerry. Please."

"Okay," he said. "I agree. You have the right to know. But you're an expert at keeping things confidential, and I assume you'll keep this a secret. Is that fair?"

"Yes."

He nodded. "When I met her, she was pregnant. She told me the father was someone I didn't know—that was true then—and that she wasn't going to return to him."

It was fifteen years, but it still hurt.

"She offered me a choice," he said. "If I wanted to know more about it she'd answer all my questions. Or I could accept him—and her. I never found that hard to do. We never went through an adoption, never had to. As far as anyone knew, he was mine. Yes, you're his father. We never told him anything about it. That was the way she wanted it. Once I understood it, I wanted it too."

She was pregnant the day she broke it off with us. I let it sink in, go through me. As it did, the questions I'd had for years fell away. She was afraid of the risk of making a life with me, but it wasn't her own life she was concerned about. She made a sacrifice, traded love for what was good for someone else, someone more important than either of us. And, of course, he was. And she knew something else: If I'd known she was pregnant, I'd never have left. And that would have hurt all of us in the end. Which explains why she was so resolute, so unbending and clear when she told me we had to go our separate ways. It wasn't out of coldness, which was how it felt. It was out of love.

"It was over between Karen and me before she ever met you." I was going to say some more. He stopped me.

"Don't," he said. "She had a life before we met. She was entitled to one. There's nothing to explain."

"But then I came back, as a friend."

"It's what she wanted," he said. "It was hard at first. But she wanted you around. In his life in some way. In hers. Maybe in mine. She had a way of holding on to people, the good ones. I think she was still friends with everyone she liked all her life."

Neither of us said anything for a while. It was like the moment of silence they ask you to have when you honor the dead. But nobody had to ask.

"What's best for him is all that matters," I said. "I think you and Karen were right to keep it a secret."

"Hard for you," he said.

I couldn't disagree. We said good night and I went home. I needed to be alone.

CHAPTER THIRTY - ONE

On a Saturday morning in early June I woke up at four. It was earlier than I ever like to wake up. But to get to the Caribbean from Philadelphia, there isn't much choice. To go to one of the southern islands, you have to be out of the city by seven. I was on my way to Dominica, as rustic as the Caribbean gets. The beaches are black volcanic sand, the water is cut-glass clear. And if you believe the tribal marketers, there is a waterfall for every day of the year. My share of Hartman's pot of gold was more than enough to finance the trip.

Two weeks with nothing to do had helped. I spent much of the time with Rachel. We helped each other sort some things out. I also learned that she wasn't rich. She had used most of her court winnings to help out her poorer clients and donated the rest to good causes.

The best part of the way things ended up was that everyone was getting paid. The estate of James M. Hartman was in the process of being probated under the judge's skillful guidance. A check for five hundred thousand had already arrived at Jerry's house. And checks of various sizes would soon go to all the other families on the list.

I hadn't taken any steps to see that Mrs. Stein learned the truth or that any of the other victims' families did. I didn't see how it would help them to know.

I was looking out the floor-to-ceiling window as the ground crews were working on the plane. I heard my name. Rachel had arrived.

"Can't say I've traveled too much," she said. "Is this one of those islands where they greet you by hanging plants around your neck?"

"Not exactly. But they have warm sunshine every day, green mountains that rise straight up out of the ocean, and lots of privacy."

"Beats a wreath," she said.

The overhead announcement said our plane was ready to board. We picked up our carry-ons and walked toward the gate. She put her arm in mine. I was thinking about Sean, and Karen's choice. I would have to learn to live with the choices we all had made. I considered myself an expert at the secrets people kept. I used secrets to make things right, and to get my way. I had a son, but for a long time that had been a secret to me. Fifteen years. And Sean would never know. The woman I was with was even more familiar than I with secrets and what they could cost. Somehow, she had learned to survive. There was much I could learn from her, but that too would take time.

We boarded the plane. The Caribbean was a good place to start.

Philip Harper is the pseudonym for two veteran investigators. Jonathan Neumann heads an investigative reporting team at the *Philadelphia Inquirer* and has worked on five different Pulitzer Prize-winning stories. He lives in Montgomery County, Pennsylvania. Stuart Green is a seasoned psychologist who spent years working with violent offenders for the courts of New York City. He lives in Union County, New Jersey. Their previous Gray novels were *Payback* and *Final Fear.*